PENGUIN CLASSICS
The Grand Banks Café

'I love reading Simenon. He makes ⸺
— William Faulkner

'A truly wonderful writer . . . marvellously readable – lucid, simple, absolutely in tune with the world he creates'
— Muriel Spark

'Few writers have ever conveyed with such a sure touch, the bleakness of human life'
— A. N. Wilson

'One of the greatest writers of the twentieth century . . . Simenon was unequalled at making us look inside, though the ability was masked by his brilliance at absorbing us obsessively in his stories'
— *Guardian*

'A novelist who entered his fictional world as if he were part of it'
— Peter Ackroyd

'The greatest of all, the most genuine novelist we have had in literature'
— André Gide

'Superb . . . The most addictive of writers . . . A unique teller of tales'
— *Observer*

'The mysteries of the human personality are revealed in all their disconcerting complexity'
— Anita Brookner

'A writer who, more than any other crime novelist, combined a high literary reputation with popular appeal' — P. D. James

'A supreme writer . . . Unforgettable vividness' — *Independent*

'Compelling, remorseless, brilliant'
— John Gray

'Extraordinary masterpieces of the twentieth century'
— John Banville

GEORGES SIMENON

The Grand Banks Café

Translated by DAVID COWARD

PENGUIN BOOKS

PENGUIN CLASSICS

Published by the Penguin Group
Penguin Books Ltd, 80 Strand, London WC2R ORL, England
Penguin Group (USA) Inc., 375 Hudson Street, New York, New York 10014, USA
Penguin Group (Canada), 90 Eglinton Avenue East, Suite 700, Toronto, Ontario, Canada M4P 2Y3
(a division of Pearson Penguin Canada Inc.)
Penguin Ireland, 25 St Stephen's Green, Dublin 2, Ireland (a division of Penguin Books Ltd)
Penguin Group (Australia), 707 Collins Street, Melbourne, Victoria 3008, Australia
(a division of Pearson Australia Group Pty Ltd)
Penguin Books India Pvt Ltd, 11 Community Centre, Panchsheel Park, New Delhi – 110 017, India
Penguin Group (NZ), 67 Apollo Drive, Rosedale, Auckland 0632, New Zealand
(a division of Pearson New Zealand Ltd)
Penguin Books (South Africa) (Pty) Ltd, Block D, Rosebank Office Park, 181 Jan Smuts Avenue,
Parktown North, Gauteng 2193, South Africa
Penguin Books Ltd, Registered Offices: 80 Strand, London WC2R ORL, England

www.penguin.com

First published in French as *Au Rendez-Vous des Terre-Neuvas* by Fayard 1931
This translation first published 2014

015

Copyright 1931 by Georges Simenon Limited
Translation copyright © David Coward, 2014
GEORGES SIMENON ® Simenon.tm
MAIGRET ® Georges Simenon Limited
All rights reserved

The moral rights of the author and translator have been asserted

Set in 12.5/15pt Dante MT Std
Typeset by Palimpsest Book Production Ltd, Falkirk, Stirlingshire

Printed and bound in Great Britain by Clays Ltd, Elcograf S.p.A.

ISBN: 978-0-141-39350-6

www.greenpenguin.co.uk

1. *The Glass Eater*

... that he's the finest young man around here there ever was, and that all this could well be the death of his mother. He's all she's got. I am absolutely sure that he's innocent: everybody here is. But the sailors I've talked to reckon he'll be found guilty because civilian courts never understand anything to do with the sea.

Do everything you can, old friend, just as if you were doing it for me. I see from the papers that you've become something very important in the Police Judiciaire, and ...

It was a June morning. The windows of the flat on Boulevard Richard-Lenoir were wide open. Madame Maigret was finishing packing large wicker trunks, and Maigret, who was not wearing a collar, was reading aloud.

'Who's it from?'

'Jorissen. We were at school together. He's a primary-school teacher now in Quimper. Listen, are you still set on passing our week's holiday in Alsace?'

She stared at him, not understanding. The question was so unexpected. For the past twenty years they'd always spent their holidays with family, and always in the same village in eastern France.

'What if we went to stay by the sea instead?'

He read out parts of the letter again, in a half whisper:

. . . you are better placed than I am to get accurate information. Very briefly, Pierre Le Clinche, aged twenty, a former pupil of mine, sailed three months ago on the *Océan*, a Fécamp trawler which was going fishing for cod off Newfoundland. The boat docked back in port yesterday. Hours later, the body of the captain was found floating in the harbour, and all the signs point to foul play. Pierre Le Clinche is the man who's been arrested.

'We'll be able to take it just as easy at Fécamp as anywhere else!' said Maigret, holding out no great hopes.

Objections were raised. In Alsace, Madame Maigret was with her family and helped with making jam and plum brandy. The thought of staying in a hotel by the seaside with a lot of other people from Paris filled her with dread.

'What would I do all day?'

In the end, she packed her sewing and her crocheting.

'Just don't expect me to go swimming! I thought I'd better warn you in advance.'

They had arrived at the Hôtel de la Plage at five. Once there, Madame Maigret had set about rearranging the room to her liking. Then they'd had dinner.

Later, Maigret, now alone, pushed open the frosted-glass door of a harbour-front café, the Grand Banks Café.

It was located opposite the berth where the trawler the *Océan* was tied up, just by a line of railway trucks. Acetylene lamps hung from the rigging, and in their raw light a number of figures were busily unloading cod, which they passed from hand to hand and piled into the trucks after the fish had been weighed.

There were ten of them at work, men and women, dirty, their clothes torn and stiff with salt. By the weighing scales stood a well-turned-out young man, with a boater over one ear and a notebook in his hand, in which he recorded the weighed catch.

A rank, stomach-churning smell, which distance did nothing to lessen, seeped into the bar, where the heat made it even more oppressive.

Maigret sat down in a free corner, on the bench seat. He was surrounded by noise and activity. There were men standing, men sitting, glasses on the marble-topped tables. All were sailors.

'What'll it be?'

'A beer.'

The serving girl went off. The landlord came up to him:

'I've got another room next door, you know. For tourists. This lot make such a din in here!' He winked. 'Well, after three months at sea, it's understandable.'

'Are these the crew of the *Océan*?'

'Most of them. The other boats aren't back yet. You mustn't pay any attention. Some of them have been drunk for three days. Are you staying put? . . . I bet you're a painter, right? We get them in now and again. They do sketches. There, see? Over the counter? One of them drew me, head and shoulders.'

But the inspector offered so little encouragement to his chatter that the landlord gave up and went away.

'A copper two-*sou* bit! Who's got a copper two-*sou* bit?'

shouted a sailor no taller than a sixteen-year-old youth and as thin.

His head was old, his face was lopsided, and he was missing a few teeth. Drink made his eyes bright, and a three-day stubble had spread over his jaws.

Someone tossed him a coin. He bent it almost double with his fingers, then put it between his teeth and snapped it in two.

'Who's wants to have a go next?'

He strutted around. He sensed that everyone was looking at him and was ready to do anything to remain the centre of attention.

As a puffy-faced mechanic produced a coin, he stepped in:

'Half a mo'. This is what you got to do as well.'

He picked up an empty glass, took a large bite out of it and chewed the broken pieces with a show of relish worthy of a gourmet.

'Ha ha!' he smirked. 'You're all welcome to give it a try . . . Fill me up again, Léon!'

He looked round the bar boastfully until his eyes came to rest on Maigret. His eyebrows came together in a deep frown.

For a moment he seemed nonplussed. Then he started to move forwards. He had to lean on a table to steady himself because he was so drunk.

'You here for me?' he blustered.

'Take it easy, Louis boy!'

'Still on about that business with the wallet? Listen, boys. You didn't believe me just now when I told you about my run-ins with the Rue de Lappe boys. Well, here's a top-notch cop who's come out of his way to see yours truly . . . Will it be all right if I have another little drink?'

All eyes were now on Maigret.

'Sit yourself down here, Louis boy, and stop playing the fool!'

Louis guffawed:

'You paying? No, that would be the day! . . . Is it all right with you, boys, if the chief inspector buys me a drink? . . . Make it brandy, Léon, a large one!'

'Were you on the *Océan*?'

The change in Louis was instant. His face darkened so much that it seemed as if he had suddenly sobered up. He shifted his position on the bench seat, backing off suspiciously.

'What if I was?'

'Nothing . . . Cheers . . . Been drunk long?'

'We been celebrating for three days. Ever since we landed. I gave my pay to Léon. Nine hundred francs, give or take. Here until it runs out . . . How much have I got left, Léon, you old crook?'

'Well, not enough for you to go on buying rounds until tomorrow! About fifty francs. Isn't it a stupid shame, inspector! Tomorrow he'll be skint and he'll have to sign as a stoker on the first boat that'll have him. It's the same story every time. Mark you, I don't encourage them to drink! The very opposite!'

'Shut your mouth!'

The others had lost their high spirits. They talked in whispers and kept looking round at the table where the inspector was sitting.

'Are all these men from the *Océan*?'

'All save the big fellow in the cap, who's a pilot, and the one with ginger hair. He's a ship's carpenter.'

'Tell me what happened.'

'I got nothing to say.'

'Watch your step, Louis! Don't forget the wallet business, which ended up with you doing your glass-eating number behind bars.'

'All I'd get is three months, and anyway I could do with a rest. But if you want, why not just lock me up right now?'

'Were you working in the engine room?'

'Sure! As usual! I was second fireman.'

'Did you see much of the captain?'

'Maybe twice in all.'

'And the wireless operator?'

'Dunno.'

'Léon! Same again.'

Louis gave a contemptuous laugh.

'I could be drunk as a lord and still I wouldn't tell you anything I didn't want to say. But since you're here, you could offer to buy the boys a round. After the lousy trip like the one we just been on!'

A sailor, not yet twenty, approached shiftily and tugged Louis' sleeve. They both started talking in Breton.

'What did he say?'

'He said it's time I went to bed.'

'A friend of yours?'

Louis shrugged, and just as the young sailor was about to take his glass off him, he downed it in one defiant gulp.

The Breton had thick eyebrows and wavy hair.

'Sit down with us,' said Maigret.

But without replying the sailor moved to another table, where he sat staring unblinkingly at both of them.

The atmosphere was heavy and sour. The sounds of tourists playing dominoes came from the next room, which was lighter and cleaner.

'Catch much cod?' asked Maigret who pursued his line of thought with the single-mindedness of a mechanical drill.

'It was no good. When we landed, it was half rotten!'

'How come?'

'Not enough salt! . . . Or too much! . . . It was off! There'll not be a third of the crew who'll go out on her again next week.'

'Is the *Océan* going out again?'

'By God, yes! Otherwise what's the point of boats with engines? Sailboats go out the once, from February to October. But these trawlers can fit in two trips to the Grand Banks.'

'Are you going back on her?'

Louis spat on the floor and gave a weary shrug.

'I'd just as well be banged up at Fresnes . . . You must be joking!'

'And the captain?'

'I got nothing to say!'

He had lit the stump of a cigar he'd found lying about. Suddenly he retched, made a rush for the door and could be seen throwing up on the kerb, where the Breton joined him.

'It's a crying shame,' sighed the landlord. 'The day before yesterday, he had nearly a thousand francs in his pocket. Today, it's touch and go if he doesn't end up owing me money! Oysters and lobster! And that's not reckoning all the drinks he stood everybody, as if he didn't know what to do with his money.'

'Did you know the wireless operator on the *Océan*?'

'He had a room here. As a matter of fact, he'd eat his dinners off this very table and then he'd go off to write in the room next door because it was quieter there.'

'Write to who?'

'Not just letters . . . Looked like poetry or novels. A kid with an education, well brought up. Now that I know you're police, I can tell you that it was a mistake when your lot . . .'

'Even though the captain had been killed?'

A shrug for an answer. The landlord sat down facing Maigret. Louis came back in, made straight for the counter and ordered another drink. His companion, still talking Breton, continued to tell him to stay calm.

'Pay no attention . . . Once they're back on dry land, they're like that: they booze, they shout, they fight, they break windows. On board they work like the devil. Even Louis! The chief mechanic on the *Océan* was telling me only yesterday that he does the work of two men . . . When they were at sea, a steam joint split. Repairing it was danger-ous . . . No one wanted to do it . . . But Louis stepped up to the mark . . . If you keep him away from the bottle . . .'

Léon lowered his voice and ran his eyes over his custom-ers suspiciously.

'Maybe this time they've got different reasons for going on the bottle. They won't tell you anything, not you!

Because you're not a seafaring man. But I overhear them talking. I used to be a pilot. There are things . . .'

'What things?'

'It's hard to explain . . . You know that there aren't enough men in Fécamp to crew all the trawlers. So they bring them in from Brittany. Those boys have their own way of looking at things, they're a superstitious lot . . .'

He lowered his voice even further, until he was barely audible.

'It seems that this time they had the evil eye. It started in port, even before they sailed. There was this sailor who'd climbed the derrick to wave to his wife . . . He was hanging on to a rope, which broke, and the next moment he's lying on deck with his leg in a hell of a mess! They had to ferry him ashore in a dory. And then there was the ship's boy who didn't want to go to sea, he was bawling and yelling! Then three days later, they telegraphed saying he'd been washed overboard by a wave! A kid of fifteen! A small lad with fair hair, skinny he was, with a girlish name: Jean-Marie. And that wasn't all . . . Julie, bring us a couple of glasses of calvados . . . The right-hand bottle . . . No, not that one . . . The one with the glass stopper . . .'

'So the evil eye went on?'

'I don't know exactly. It's as if they're all too scared to talk about it. Even so, if the wireless operator has been arrested, it's because the police must have got to hear that during the whole time they were at sea he and the captain never said a word to each other . . . They were like oil and vinegar.'

'And?'

'Things happened . . . Things that don't make any sense.

Like for instance when the skipper made them move the boat to a position where no one ever heard of cod being caught! And he went berserk when the head fisherman refused to do what he was told! He got his revolver out. It was like they were off their heads! For a whole month they didn't even net a ton of fish! And then all of a sudden, the fishing was good. But even then, the cod had to be sold at half price because it hadn't been kept right. And on it went. Even when they were coming into the harbour, they lost control twice and sank a rowing boat. It was like there was a curse on the boat. Then the skipper sent all hands ashore without leaving anyone on watch and stayed on board that evening all by himself.

'It was around nine o'clock. They were all in here getting drunk. The wireless operator went up to his room. Then he went out. He was seen heading in the direction of the boat.

'It was then that it happened. A fisherman down in the harbour who was getting ready to leave heard a noise like something falling in the water.

'He ran to see, with a customs man he'd met on the way. They lit lanterns . . . There was a body in the water. It had caught in the *Océan*'s anchor chain.

'It was the skipper! He was dead when they fished him out. They tried artificial respiration. They couldn't understand it. He hadn't been in the water ten minutes.

'The doctor explained the reason. Seems as how somebody had strangled him *before* . . . Do you follow me? And they found the wireless operator on board in his cabin, which is just astern of the funnel. You can see it from here.

'The police came here and searched his room. They found some burned papers . . .

'What do you make of it? . . . Ho! Julie, two calvados! . . . Your very good health!'

Louis, getting more and more carried away, had gripped a chair with his teeth and, in the middle of a circle of sailors, was holding it horizontally while staring defiantly at Maigret.

'Was the captain from around here?' asked the inspector.

'That he was. A curious sort. Not much taller or wider than Louis. But always polite, always friendly. And always nattily turned out. I don't think he went much to cafés. He wasn't married. He had digs in Rue d'Étretat, with a widow whose husband had worked for customs. There was talk that they'd get wed in the end. He'd been fishing off Newfoundland these fifteen years. Always for the same owners: the French Cod Company. Captain Fallut, to give him his full name. They're in a fix now if they want to send the *Océan* out to the Grand Banks. No captain! And half the crew not wanting to sign on for another tour!'

'Why is that?'

'Don't try to understand! The evil eye, like I told you. There's talk of laying the boat up until next year. On top of which the police have told the crew they have to stay available.'

'And the wireless operator is behind bars?'

'Yes. They took him away the same evening, in handcuffs he was . . . I was standing in the doorway. I tell you God's truth, the wife cried . . . and so did I. But he wasn't a special customer. I used to knock a bit off when I sold him supplies. He wasn't much of a drinker himself.'

They were interrupted by a sudden uproar. Louis had thrown himself at the Breton, presumably because the Breton had insisted on trying to stop him drinking. Both were rolling around on the floor. The others got out of their way.

It was Maigret who separated them, picking them up one in each hand.

'That's enough! You want to argue?'

The scuffle was over quickly. The Breton, whose hands were free, pulled a knife from his pocket. The inspector saw it just in time and with a swift back heel sent it spinning two metres away.

The shoe caught the Breton on the chin, which started to bleed. Louis, still in a daze and still drunk, rushed to his friend and started crying and saying he was sorry.

Léon came up to Maigret. He had his watch in his hand.

'Time I closed up! If I don't we'll have the police on the doorstep. Every evening it's the same story! I just can't kick them out!'

'Do they sleep on board the *Océan*?'

'Yes. Unless, that is, and it happened to two of them yesterday, they sleep where they fall, in the gutter. I found them this morning when I opened the shutters.'

The serving girl went round gathering glasses off the tables. The men drifted off in groups of two or three. Only Louis and the Breton didn't budge.

'Need a room?' Léon asked Maigret.

'No thanks. I'm booked into the Hôtel de la Plage.'

'Can I say something?'

'What?'

'It isn't that I want to give you advice. It's none of my business. But if anyone was feeling sorry for the wireless operator, maybe it wouldn't be a bad idea to *chercher la femme*, as they say in books. I've heard a few whispers along those lines . . .'

'Did Pierre Le Clinche have a girlfriend?'

'What, him? No fear! He'd got himself engaged wherever it was he came from. Every day he'd write home, letters six pages long.'

'Who do you mean, then?'

'I dunno. Maybe it's more complicated than people think. Besides . . .'

'Besides what?'

'Nothing. Behave yourself, Louis! Go home to bed!'

But Louis was far too drunk for that. He was tearful, he had his arms around his friend, whose chin was still bleeding, and he kept saying sorry.

Maigret left the bar, hands thrust deep in his pockets and with his collar turned up, for the air was cool.

In the vestibule of the Hôtel de la Plage, he saw a young woman sitting in a wicker chair. A man got up from another chair and smiled. There was a slight awkwardness in his smile.

It was Jorissen, the primary-school teacher from Quimper. Maigret had not seen him for fifteen years, and Jorissen was not sure whether he should treat him with their old easy familiarity.

'Look, I'm sorry . . . I . . . that is we, Mademoiselle

Léonnec and I, have only just got here . . . I did the rounds of the hotels . . . They said you . . . they said you'd be back . . . She's Pierre Le Clinche's fiancée . . . She insisted . . .'

She was tall, rather pale, rather shy. But when Maigret shook her hand, he sensed that behind the façade of small-town, unsophisticated coyness there was a strong will.

She didn't speak. She felt out of her depth. As did Jorissen, who was still just a primary-school teacher who was now meeting up again with his old friend, who now held one of the highest ranks in the Police Judiciare.

'They pointed out Madame Maigret in the lounge just now, but I didn't like to . . .'

Maigret took a closer look at the girl, who was neither pretty nor plain, but there was something touching about her natural simplicity.

'You do know that he's innocent, don't you?' she said finally, looking at no one in particular.

The porter was waiting to get back to his bed. He had already unbuttoned his jacket.

'We'll see about that tomorrow . . . Have you got a room somewhere?'

'I've got the room next to you . . . to yours,' stammered the teacher from Quimper, still unsure of himself. 'And Mademoiselle Léonnec is on the floor above . . . I've got to get back tomorrow, there are exams on . . . Do you think . . . ?'

'Tomorrow! We'll see then,' Maigret said again.

And as he was getting ready for bed, his wife, already half asleep, murmured:

'Don't forget to turn the light out.'

2. The Tan-Coloured Shoes

Side by side, not looking at each other, they walked together first along the beach, which was deserted at that time of day, and then along the quays by the harbour.

Gradually, the silences grew fewer until Marie Léonnec was speaking in a more or less natural tone of voice.

'You'll see! You'll like him straight away! He couldn't be anything but likeable! And then you'll understand that . . .'

Maigret kept shooting curious, admiring glances at her. Jorissen had gone back to Quimper, very early that morning, leaving the girl by herself in Fécamp.

'I can't make her come with me,' he had said. 'She's far too independent for that.'

The previous evening, she was as unforthcoming as a young woman raised in the peace and quiet of a small town can be. Now, it wasn't an hour since she and Maigret had walked out of the Hôtel de la Plage together.

The inspector was behaving in his most crusty manner.

But to no effect. She refused to let herself be intimidated. She was not taken in by him, and she smiled confidently.

'His only fault,' she went on, 'is that he is so very sensitive. But it's hardly surprising. His father was just a poor fisherman, and for years his mother mended nets to raise him. Now he keeps her. He's educated. He's got a bright future before him.'

'Are your parents well off?' Maigret asked bluntly.

'They are the biggest makers of ropes and metal cables in Quimper. That's why Pierre wouldn't even speak to my father about us. For a whole year, we saw each other in secret.'

'You were both over eighteen?'

'Just. I was the one who told my parents. Pierre swore that he wouldn't marry me until he was earning at least two thousand francs a month. So you see . . .'

'Has he written to you since he was arrested?'

'Just one letter. It was very short. And that from someone who used to send me a letter pages and pages long every day! He said it would be best for me and my parents if I told everyone back home that it was all over between us.'

They passed near the *Océan*, which was still being unloaded. It was high tide, and its black hull dominated the wharves. In the foredeck three men stripped to the waist were getting washed. Among them Maigret recognized Louis.

He also noticed a gesture: one of the men nudged the third man with his shoulder and nodded towards Maigret and the girl. Maigret scowled.

'Just shows how considerate he is!' continued the voice at his side. 'He knows how quickly scandal spreads in a small town like Quimper. He wanted to give me back my freedom.'

The morning was clear. The girl, in her grey two-piece suit, looked like a student or a primary-school teacher.

'For my parents to have let me come here, they must

obviously trust him too. But my father would prefer me to marry someone in business.'

At the police station Maigret left her in the waiting room, sitting some considerable time in the waiting room. He jotted down a few notes.

Half an hour later, they both walked into the jail.

It was Maigret in his surly mood, hands behind his back, pipe clenched between his teeth, shoulders bent, who now stood in one corner of the cell. He had informed the authorities that he was not taking an official interest in the investigation, that he was following its progress out of curiosity.

Several people had described the wireless operator to him, and the picture he had formed corresponded exactly to the young man he was now seeing in the flesh.

He was tall and slim, in a conventional suit, though a little on the shabby side, with the half-solemn, half-timid look about him of a schoolboy who is always top of his class. There were freckles on his cheeks. His hair was cropped short.

He had started when the door was opened. For a moment, he stayed well away from the girl who walked straight up to him. She had had to throw herself into his arms, literally, and cling on hard while he looked around in bewilderment.

'Marie! . . . Who on earth . . . ? How . . . ?'

He was quite disoriented. But he wasn't the sort to get excited. The lenses of his glasses clouded over, that was all. His lips trembled.

17

'You shouldn't have come.'

He caught sight of Maigret, whom he didn't know, and then stared at the door, which had been left half-open.

He wasn't wearing a collar, and there were no laces in his shoes. He also had a beard, gingerish and several days old. He was still feeling awkward about these things, despite the sudden shock he'd had. He felt his bare neck and his prominent Adam's apple with an embarrassed movement of his hand.

'Is my mother . . . ?'

'She didn't come. But she doesn't think you're guilty any more than I do.'

The girl was no more able than he was to give vent to her feelings. The moment fell flat. Maybe it was the intimidating effect of the surroundings.

They looked at each other and, not knowing what to say, groped for words. Then Mademoiselle Léonnec turned and pointed to Maigret.

'He's a friend of Jorissen's. He's a detective chief inspector in the Police Judiciaire and he's agreed to help us.'

Le Clinche hesitated about offering his hand, then did not dare to.

'Thanks . . . I . . .'

Another moment that failed entirely. The girl knew it and felt like crying. She had been counting on a touching interview which would win Maigret over to their side.

She gave her fiancé a look of resentment, even of muted impatience.

'You must tell him everything that might help your defence.'

Pierre Le Clinche sighed, ill at ease and unsettled.

'I've just a few questions for you,' the inspector broke in. 'All the crew say that throughout the voyage your dealings with the captain were more than cool. And yet, when you sailed, you were on good terms with him. What happened to bring about the change?'

The wireless operator opened his mouth, said nothing, then stared at the floor, looking very sorry for himself.

'Something to do with your duties? For the first two days, you ate with the first mate and the chief mechanic. After that you preferred to eat with the men.'

'Yes . . . I know . . .'

'Why?'

Losing patience, Marie Léonnec said:

'Out with it, Pierre! We're trying to save you! You must tell the truth.'

'I don't know.'

He looked limp, cowed, almost without hope.

'Did you have any differences of opinion with Captain Fallut?'

'No.'

'And yet you lived with him for nearly three months cooped up on the same ship without ever saying a single word to him. Everybody noticed. Some of them talked behind his back, saying that there were times when Fallut gave the impression of being mad.'

'I don't know.'

It was all Marie Léonnec could do to choke back her frustration.

'When the *Océan* returned to port, you went ashore

with the others. When you got to your room, you burned a number of papers . . .'

'Yes. Nothing of any importance.'

'You keep a regular journal in which you write down everything you see. Wasn't what you burned your journal of the voyage?'

Le Clinche remained standing, head down, like a schoolboy who hasn't done his homework and keeps his eyes stubbornly on his feet.

'Yes.'

'Why?'

'I don't remember!'

'And you can't remember why you went back on board either? Though not straight away. You were seen crouching behind a truck fifty metres from the boat.'

The girl looked at the inspector, then at her fiancé, then back to the inspector and began to feel out of her depth.

'Yes.'

'The captain walked down the gangplank on to the quay. It was at that moment that he was attacked.'

Pierre Le Clinche still said nothing.

'Talk to me, dammit!'

'Yes, answer him, Pierre! We're trying to save you. I don't understand . . . I . . .'

Her eyes filled with tears.

'Yes.'

'Yes what?'

'I was there!'

'And you saw?'

'Not clearly . . . There were a lot of barrels, trucks . . .

Two men fighting, then one running off and a body falling into the water.'

'What was the man who ran away like?'

'I don't know . . .'

'Was he dressed like a sailor?'

'No!'

'So you know how he was dressed?'

'All I noticed was a pair of tan-coloured shoes under a gas lamp as he ran away.'

'What did you do next?'

'I went on board.'

'Why? And why didn't you try to save the captain? Did you know he was already dead?'

A heavy silence. Marie Léonnec clasped both hands together in anguish.

'Speak, Pierre! Speak . . . please!'

'Yes . . . No . . . I swear I don't know!'

Footsteps in the corridor. It was the custody officer coming to say that they were ready for Le Clinche in the examining magistrate's office.

His fiancée stepped forward, intending to kiss him. He hesitated. In the end, he put his arms round her, slowly, deliberately.

So it was not her lips that he kissed but the fine, fair curls at her temples.

'Pierre!'

'You shouldn't have come!' he told her, his brow furrowed, as he wearily followed the custody officer out.

Maigret and Marie Léonnec returned to the exit without speaking. Outside she sighed unhappily:

'I don't understand . . . I . . .'

Then, holding her head high:

'But he's innocent, I know he is! We don't understand because we've never been in a predicament like his. For three days he's been behind bars, and everybody thinks he's guilty! . . . He's a very shy person . . .'

Maigret was moved, for she was doing her level best to make her words sound positive and convincing, though inside she was utterly devastated.

'You will do something to help despite everything, won't you?'

'On condition that you go back home, to Quimper.'

'No! . . . I won't! . . . Look . . . Let me . . .'

'In that case, take yourself off to the beach. Go and sit by my wife and try to find something to do. She's bound to have something you can sew.'

'What are you going to do? Do you think the tan-coloured shoes are a clue? . . .'

People turned and stared at them, for Marie Léonnec was waving her arms about, and it looked as if they were having an argument.

'Let me say it again: I'll do everything in my power . . . Look, this street leads straight to the Hôtel de la Plage. Tell my wife that I might be back late for lunch.'

He turned on his heel and walked as far as the quays. His surly manner had disappeared. He was almost smiling. He'd been afraid there might have been a stormy scene in the cell, heated protests, tears, kisses. But it had passed off very differently, in a way that was more straightforward, more harrowing and more significant.

He had liked the boy, more precisely the part of him that was distant, withdrawn.

As he passed a shop, he ran into Louis, who was holding a pair of gumboots in his hand.

'And where are you off to?'

'To sell these. Do you want to buy them? It's the best thing they make in Canada. I defy you to find anything as good in France. Two hundred francs . . .'

Even so Louis seemed a touch jittery and was only waiting for the nod to be on his way.

'Did you ever get the idea that Captain Fallut was crazy?'

'You don't see much down in a coal bunker, you know.'

'But you do talk. So?'

'There were weird stories going round, of course.'

'What stories?'

'All sorts! . . . Something and nothing! . . . It's hard to put your finger on it. Especially when you're back on dry land again.'

He was still holding the boots in his hand, and the owner of the ship's chandler's shop who had seen him coming, was waiting for him in his doorway.

'Do you need me any more?'

'When did those stories start exactly?'

'Oh, straight away. A ship is in good shape or it's in poor shape. I tell you: the *Océan* was sick as a dog.'

'Handling errors?'

'And how! What can I say? Things that don't make any sense, though they happen right enough! The fact is we had this feeling we'd never see port again . . . Look, is it

23

true that I won't be bothered again over that business with the wallet?'

'We'll see.'

The port was almost empty. In summer, all the boats are at sea off Newfoundland, except the smaller fishing vessels which go out after fresh fish in coastal waters. There was only the dark shape of the *Océan* to be seen in the harbour, and it was the *Océan* that filled the air with a strong smell of cod.

Near the trucks was a man in leather gaiters. On his head was a cap with a silk tassel.

'The boat's owner?' Maigret asked a passing customs man.

'Yes. He's head of French Cod.'

The inspector introduced himself. The man looked at him suspiciously but without taking his eyes off the unloading operation.

'What do you make of the murder of your captain?'

'What do I think about it? I think that there's 800 tons of cod that's off, that if this nonsense goes on, the boat won't be going out again for a second voyage, that it's not the police who'll sort out the mess or cover the losses!'

'I assume you had every confidence in Captain Fallut?'

'Yes. And?'

'Do you think the wireless operator . . . ?'

'The wireless operator is neither here nor there: it's a whole year down the chute! And that's not counting the nets they came back with! Those nets cost two million francs, you know! Full of holes, as if someone has been having fun fishing up rocks! On top of which, the crew's been going on about the evil eye! . . . Hoy, you there! What do you think you're playing at? . . . God give me strength! Did I or did I not tell you to finish loading that truck first?'

And he started running alongside the boat, swearing at all the hands.

Maigret stayed a few moments more, watching the boat being unloaded. Then he moved off in the direction of the jetty, where there were groups of fishermen in pink canvas jerkins.

He'd been there only a moment when a voice behind him said:

'Hoy! Inspector!'

It was Léon, the landlord of the Grand Banks Café, who was trying to catch him up by pumping his short legs as fast as he could.

'Come and have a drink in the bar.'

He was behaving mysteriously. It seemed promising. As they walked, he explained:

'It's all calmed down now. The boys who haven't gone home to Brittany or the villages round about have just about spent all their money. I've only had a few mackerel men in all morning.'

They walked across the quays and went into the café, which was empty except for the girl from behind the bar, who was wiping tables.

'Half a mo'. What'll you have? Aperitif? . . . It's almost time for one . . . Not that, as I told you yesterday, I encourage the boys to drink too much . . . The opposite! . . . I mean, when they've had a drop or three, they start smashing the place up, and that costs me more than I make out of them . . . Julie! Pop into the kitchen and see if I'm there!'

He gave the inspector a knowing wink.

'Your very good health! . . . I saw you in the distance and since I had something to tell you . . .'

He crossed the room to make sure the girl was not listening behind the door. And then, looking even more mysterious and pleased with himself, he took something out of his pocket, a piece of card about the size of a photo.

'There! What do you make of that!'

It was indeed a photo, a picture of a woman. But the face was completely hidden, scribbled all over in red ink. Someone had tried to obliterate the head, someone very angry. The pen had bitten into the paper. There were so many criss-crossed lines that not a single square millimetre had been left visible.

On the other hand, below the head, the torso had not been touched. A pair of large breasts. A light-coloured silk dress, very tight and very low cut.

'Where did you get this?'

More knowing winks.

'Since there's just the two of us, I can tell you . . . Le Clinche's sea-chest doesn't fasten properly, so he'd got into the habit of sliding his girlfriend's letters under the cloth on his table.'

'And you used to read them?'

'They were of no interest to me . . . No, it was luck . . . When the place was searched, nobody thought of looking under the tablecloth. It came to me last night, and that's what I found. Of course, you can't see the face. But it's obviously not the girlfriend, she isn't stacked like that! Anyway, I've seen a photo of her. So there's another woman lurking in the background.'

Maigret stared at the photo. The line of the shoulders was inviting. The woman was probably younger than Marie Léonnec. And there was something extremely sensual about those breasts.

But also something vulgar too. The dress looked shop-bought. Seduction on the cheap.

'Is there any red ink in the house?'

'No! Just green.'

'Did Le Clinche never use red ink?'

'No. He had his own ink, on account of having a fountain pen. Special ink. Blue-black.'

Maigret stood up and made for the door.

'Do you mind excusing . . . ?'

Moments later he was on board the *Océan*, searching first the wireless operator's cabin and then the captain's, which was dirty and full of clutter.

There was no red ink anywhere on the trawler. None of the fishermen had ever seen any there.

When he left the boat, Maigret came in for sour looks from the man in gaiters, who was still bawling at his men.

'Do you use red ink in any of your offices?'

'Red ink? What for? We're not running a school . . .'

But suddenly, as if he'd just remembered something:

'Fallut was the only one who ever wrote in red ink, when he was working at home, in Rue d'Étretat. But what's all this about now? . . . You down there, watch out for that truck! All we need now is an accident! . . . So what are you after now with your red ink?'

'Nothing . . . Much obliged.'

Louis reappeared bootless and a few sheets to the wind, with a roughneck's cap on his head and a pair of scuffed shoes on his feet.

3. The Headless Photograph

. . . and that no one could tell me to my face and that I've got savings, which are at least the equivalent of a captain's pay.

Maigret left Madame Bernard standing on the doorstep of her small house in Rue d'Étretat. She was about fifty, very well preserved, and she had just spoken for a full half-hour about her first husband, about being a widow, about the captain, whom she had taken as her lodger, about the rumours which had circulated about their relationship and, finally, about an unnamed female who was beyond a shadow of a doubt a 'loose woman'.

The inspector had looked round the whole house, which was well kept but full of objects in rather bad taste. Captain Fallut's room was still as it had been arranged in readiness for his return.

Few personal possessions: some clothes in a trunk, a handful of books, mostly adventure yarns, and pictures of boats.

All redolent of an uneventful, unremarkable life.

'. . . It was understood though not finally settled, but we both knew that we would eventually get married. I would bring the house, furniture and bed linen. Nothing would have changed, and we would have been comfortably off, especially in three or four years' time, after he got his pension.'

Visible through the windows were the grocer's opposite, the road that ran down the hill and the pavement, where children were playing.

'And then this last winter he met that woman, and everything was turned upside down. At his age! How can a man lose his head over a creature like that? And he kept it all very secret. He must have been going to see her in Le Havre or somewhere, for no one here ever saw them together. I had a feeling that something was going on. He started buying more expensive underwear. And once, even a pair of silk socks! As there wasn't anything definite between us, it was none of my business, and I didn't want to look as if I was trying to defend my interests.'

The interview with Madame Bernard cast light on one whole area of the dead man's life. The small, middle-aged man who returned to port after a long tour on a trawler and spent his winters living like an upstanding citizen, with Madame Bernard, who looked after him and expected to marry him.

He ate with her, in her dining room, under a portrait of her first husband, who sported a blond moustache. Afterwards, he would go to his room and settle down with an exciting book.

And then that peace was shattered. Another woman burst on to the scene. Captain Fallut went to Le Havre frequently, took more care of his appearance, shaved more closely, even bought silk socks and hid it all from his landlady.

Still, he wasn't married, he had made no promises. He was free and yet he had never appeared once in public in Fécamp with his unknown woman.

Was it the grand passion, his belated big adventure? Or just a sordid affair?

Maigret reached the beach, saw his wife sitting in a red-striped deckchair and, just by her, Marie Léonnec, who was sewing.

There were a few bathers on the shingle, which gleamed white in the sun. A drowsy sea. And further on, on the other side of the jetty, the *Océan* at her berth, and the cargo of cod that was still being unloaded, and the resentful sailors exchanging veiled comments.

He kissed Madame Maigret on the forehead. He nodded politely to the girl and replied to her questioning look:

'Nothing special.'

His wife said in a level voice:

'Mademoiselle Léonnec has been telling me her story. Do you think that her young man is capable of doing such a thing?'

They walked slowly towards the hotel. Maigret carried both deckchairs. They were about to sit down to lunch when a uniformed policeman arrived, looking for the inspector.

'I was told to show you this, sir. It came an hour ago.'

And he held out a brown envelope, which had been already opened. There was no address on it. Inside was a sheet of paper. On it, in a tiny, thin, cramped hand, was written:

No one should be accused of bringing about my death, and no attempt should be made to understand my action.

These are my last wishes. I leave all my worldly goods to Madame Bernard, who has always been kind to me, on the condition that she sends my gold chronometer to my nephew, who is known to her, and that she sees to it that I am buried in Fécamp cemetery, near my mother.

Maigret opened his eyes wide.

'It's signed Octave Fallut!' he said in a whisper. 'How did this letter get to the police station?'

'Nobody knows, sir. It was in the letterbox. It seems that it's his handwriting right enough. The chief inspector informed the public prosecutor's department immediately.'

'Despite the fact that he was strangled! And that it is impossible to strangle yourself!' muttered Maigret.

Close by, guests who had ordered the set menu were complaining loudly about some pink radishes in a hors d'oeuvres dish.

'Wait a moment while I copy this letter. I imagine you have to take it back with you?'

'I wasn't given any special instructions but I suppose so.'

'Quite right. It must be put in the file.'

A moment or two later, Maigret, holding the copy in his hand, looked impatiently round the dining room, where he was about to waste an hour waiting for each course to arrive. All this time, Marie Léonnec had not taken her eyes off him but had not dared interrupt his grim reflections. Only Madame Maigret reacted, with a sigh, at the sight of pale cutlets.

'We'd have been better off going to Alsace.'

Maigret stood up before the dessert arrived and wiped his mouth, eager to get back to the trawler, the harbour, the fishermen. All the way there, he kept muttering:

'Fallut knew he was going to die! But did he know he would be killed? Was he trying in advance to save his killer's neck? Or was it just that he intended to commit suicide? Then again, who dropped the brown envelope in the station's postbox? There was no stamp on it, no address.'

The news had already got out, for when Maigret had nearly reached the trawler, the head of French Cod called out to him with aggressive sarcasm:

'So, it seems Fallut strangled himself! Who came up with that bright idea?'

'If you've got something to say, you can tell me which of the *Océan*'s officers are still on board.'

'None of them. The first mate has gone on the spree to Paris. The chief mechanic is at home, at Yport and won't be back until they've finished unloading.'

Maigret again looked round the captain's quarters. A narrow cabin. A bed with a dirty quilt over it. A clothes press built into the bulkhead. A blue enamel coffee-pot on an oilcloth-covered table. In a corner, a pair of boots with wooden soles.

It was dark and clammy and permeated with the same acrid smell which filled the rest of the ship. Blue-striped knitted pullovers were drying on deck. Maigret nearly lost his footing as he walked across the gangway, which was slippery with the remains of fish.

'Find anything?'

The inspector gave a shrug, took yet another gloomy look at the *Océan*, then asked a customs officer how he could get to Yport.

Yport is a village built under the cliffs six kilometres from Fécamp. A handful of fishermen's cottages. The odd farm round about. A few villas, most let furnished during the summer season, and one hotel.

On the beach, another collection of bathing costumes, small children and mothers busily knitting and embroidering.

'Could you tell me where Monsieur Laberge lives?'

'The chief mechanic on the *Océan* or the farmer?'

'The mechanic.'

He was directed to a small house with a small garden round it. As he came up to the front door, which was painted green, he heard the sound of an argument coming from inside. Two voices: a man's and a woman's. But he could not make out what they were saying. He knocked.

It all went quiet. Footsteps approached. The door opened and a tall, rangy man appeared looking suspicious and cross.

'What is it?'

A woman in housekeeping clothes was quickly tidying her dishevelled hair.

'I'm from the Police Judiciaire and I'd like to ask you a few questions.'

'You'd better come in.'

A little boy was crying, and his father pushed him roughly into the adjoining room, in which Maigret caught sight of the foot of a bed.

'You can leave us to it!' Laberge snapped at his wife.

Her eyes were red with crying too. The argument must have started in the middle of their meal, for their plates were still half full.

'What do you want to know?'

'When did you last go to Fécamp?'

'This morning. I went on my bike. It's no fun having to listen to the wife going on all day. You spend months at sea, working your guts out, and when you get back . . .'

He was still angry. However, his breath smelled strongly of alcohol.

'Women! They're all the same! Jealous don't say the half of it! They imagine a man's got nothing else on his mind except running after skirts. Listen to her! That's her giving the kid a hiding, taking it out on him!'

The child could be heard yelling in the next room, and the mother's voice getting louder.

'Stop that row, you hear! . . . Just stop it!'

Judging by the sounds, the words were accompanied by slaps and thumps, for the crying started up again, with interest.

'Ah! What a life!'

'Had Captain Fallut told you he was worried about anything in particular?'

Laberge scowled at Maigret, then moved his chair.

'Who made you think he had?'

'You'd been sailing with him for a long time, hadn't you?'

'Five years.'

'On board you took your meals together.'

'Except this last time! He got the idea that he wanted

35

to eat alone, in his cabin . . . But I'd rather not talk any more about that damned trip!'

'Where were you when the crime was committed?'

'In the café, with the others . . . They must have told you.'

'Do you think the wireless operator had any reason for attacking the captain?'

Suddenly, Laberge lost his temper.

'Where are all these questions leading? What do you want me to say? Look, it wasn't my job to keep everybody in order, was it? I'm fed up to the back teeth, fed up with this business and all the rest of it! So fed up that I'm wondering if I'm going to sign up for the next tour!'

'Obviously the last one wasn't exactly a roaring success.'

Another sharp glance at Maigret.

'What are you getting at?'

'Just that everything went wrong! A ship's boy was killed. There were more accidents than usual. The fishing wasn't good, and when the cod arrived back in Fécamp it was off . . .'

'Was that my fault?'

'I'm not saying that. I merely ask if in the events at which you were present there was anything that might explain the captain's death. He was an easy-going sort, led a quiet life . . .'

The mechanic smiled mockingly but said nothing.

'Do you know anything about him that says otherwise?'

'Look, I told you I don't know anything, that I've had enough of the whole business! Is everybody trying to drive me crazy? . . . What more do you want now?'

He had it in most for his wife. She had just come back

into the room and was hurrying to the stove, where a saucepan was giving off a smell of burning.

She was about thirty-five. She wasn't pretty and she wasn't ugly.

'I'll only be a minute,' she said meekly. 'It's the dog's dinner . . .'

'Get on with it, woman! . . . Haven't you finished yet?'

And turning to Maigret:

'Shall I give you a piece of good advice? Let it alone! Fallut is well off where he is! The less said about him, the better it'll be! Now listen: I don't know anything. You can ask me questions all day, and I wouldn't have anything else to say . . . Did you get the train here? If you don't catch the one that leaves in ten minutes, you'll not get another until eight this evening.'

He had opened the door. Sunshine flooded into the room.

When he got to the doorway, the inspector asked quietly: 'Who is your wife jealous of?'

The man gritted his teeth and did not speak.

'Do you know who this is?'

Maigret held out the photo with the head obscured by the red scribble. But he kept his thumb over the face. All that was visible was the cleavage in the silk dress.

Laberge glanced up at him quickly and tried to grab the picture.

'Do you recognize her?'

'Why should I recognize her?'

His hand was still open when Maigret put the photograph back in his pocket.

'Will you be coming to Fécamp tomorrow?'

'I don't know . . . Will you be needing me?'

'No. I was just asking. Thanks for the information you gave me.'

'But I didn't tell you anything!'

Maigret had not gone ten paces from the door when it was kicked shut and voices were raised inside the house, where the argument would now start up again, even more acrimoniously.

The chief mechanic was right: there were no trains to Fécamp until eight in the evening, and Maigret, having time on his hands, was inevitably drawn to the beach, where he sat down on the terrace of a hotel.

There was the usual holiday atmosphere: red sun umbrellas, white dresses, white trousers and a group of sightseers clustered around a fishing boat that was being winched up on to the pebble beach with a capstan.

To right and left, light-coloured cliffs. Straight ahead, the sea, pale green with white combers, and the regular murmur of wavelets lapping the shoreline.

'A beer!'

The sun was hot. A family were eating ice-creams on the next table. A young man was taking photos with a Kodak, and somewhere there were the shrill voices of little girls.

Maigret allowed his eyes to wander over the view. His thoughts grew hazy, and his brain sluggishly started weaving a daydream around Captain Fallut, who became increasingly insubstantial.

'Thanks a million!'

The words went round and round in his head, not on account of their meaning, but because they had been pronounced curtly, with biting sarcasm, by a woman somewhere behind the inspector.

'But Adèle, I told you . . .'

'Shut up!'

'You're not going to start all that again . . .'

'I'll do exactly as I please!'

It was obviously a good day for arguments. First thing that morning, Maigret had encountered a man who bristled: the head man from French Cod.

At Yport, there had been that domestic scene between the Laberges. And now on the hotel terrace an unknown couple were exchanging heated words.

'Why don't you stop and think!'

'Get lost!'

'Do you think it's clever to talk like that?'

'Damn and blast you! Haven't you got the message yet? . . . Waiter, this lemonade is warm. Get me another!'

The accent was common, and the woman was speaking more loudly than was necessary.

'But you must make up your mind!' the man said.

'Just go by yourself! I told you! And leave me alone.'

'You know, what you're doing is pretty shabby.'

'So are you!'

'Me? You dare . . . Listen, if we weren't here, I don't think I'd be able to keep control of myself!'

She laughed. Much too loudly.

'You tell a girl the nicest things!'

'Be quiet! Please!'

'Why should I?'

'Because!'

'Now that really is a clever answer, I must say!'

'Are you going to shut up?'

'If I feel like it.'

'Adèle, I'm warning you I'll . . .'

'You'll what? Kick up a fuss in front of everybody? And where would that get you? People are already listening.'

'If only you'd stop and think for a moment, you'd understand.'

She sprang to her feet like someone who has had enough. Maigret had his back turned to her but saw her shadow grow bigger on the tiled floor of the terrace.

Then he saw her, from the back, as she walked off in the direction of the sea.

From behind, she was just a silhouette against the sky, which was now turning red. All Maigret could make out was that she was quite well-dressed, but not for the beach, not with silk stockings and high heels.

It was an outfit which made it difficult for her to walk elegantly over the pebble beach. At any moment she could twist an ankle, but she was furiously, stubbornly determined to forge ahead.

'Waiter, what do I owe you?'

'But I haven't brought the lemonade which the lady . . .'

'Forget it! What's the damage?'

'Nine francs fifty . . . Won't you be having dinner here?'

'No idea.'

Maigret turned round to get a sight of the man, who

was looking very awkward because he was well aware that everyone nearby had heard everything.

He was tall and flashily elegant. His eyes looked tired, and his utter frustration was written all over his face.

When he stood up, he hesitated about which way to go and in the end, trying to look as if he didn't give a damn about anything, he set off in the direction of the young woman, who was now walking along the winding edge of the sea.

'Another pair that aren't married, for sure!' said a voice at a table where three women were busy doing crochet work.

'Why couldn't they wash their dirty linen somewhere else? It's not setting the children a very good example.'

The two silhouettes joined at the water's edge. Their words were no longer audible. But the way they stood and moved made it easy to guess what was going on.

The man pleaded and threatened. The woman refused to give an inch. At one point he grabbed her by the wrist, and it seemed as if they would come to blows.

Instead, he turned his back on her and walked away quickly towards a street nearby, where he started the engine of a small grey car.

'Waiter! Another beer!'

Then Maigret noticed that the young woman had left her handbag on the table. Imitation crocodile-skin, full to bursting, brand new.

Then a shadow coming towards him on the ground. He looked up and got a front view of the owner of the handbag, who was coming back to the terrace.

The inspector gave a start. His nostrils flared slightly.

He could be wrong, of course. It was more an impression than a certainty. But he could have sworn he was looking at the person in the headless photo.

Cautiously, he took the photo out of his pocket. The woman had sat down again.

'Well, waiter? Where's my lemonade?'

'I thought . . . The gentleman said . . .'

'I ordered lemonade!'

It was the same slightly fleshy line of the neck, the same full but firm breasts, the same voluptuous buoyancy . . .

And the same style of dressing, the same taste for very glossy silk in loud colours.

Maigret dropped the photo in such a way that the woman at the next table could not fail to see it.

And see it she did. She stared at the inspector as though she were trawling through her memories. But if she was disconcerted, her feelings did not show in her face.

Five minutes, ten minutes went by. Then there was the distant thrum of an engine. It grew louder. It was the grey car heading back to the terrace. It stopped, then set off again, as though the driver could not make up his mind to drive away and not come back.

'Gaston!'

She was on her feet. She waved to the man. This time she grasped her bag firmly and the next moment she was getting into the car.

The three women at the next table followed her with their eyes and a disapproving air. The young man with the Kodak turned round.

The grey car was already vanishing in a roar of acceleration.

'Waiter! Where can I get hold of a car?'

'I don't think you'll find one in Yport . . . There is one which sometimes takes people to Fécamp or Étretat, but now that I think I saw it drive off this morning with some English people in it.'

The inspector's thick fingers drummed rapidly on the tabletop.

'Bring me a road map. And get me the chief inspector of Fécamp police on the phone . . . Have you ever seen those two before?'

'The couple who were arguing? Almost every day this week. Yesterday they had lunch here. I think they're from Le Havre.'

There were now only families left on the beach, which exuded all the warmth of a summer evening. A black ship moved imperceptibly across the line of the horizon, entered the sun and emerged on the other side, as if it had jumped through a paper hoop.

4. *The Mark of Rage*

'Speaking for myself,' said the chief inspector of Fécamp's police department as he sharpened a blue pencil, 'I'll admit I have few illusions left. It's so rarely that we manage to clear up any of these cases involving sailors. And that's being optimistic! Just you try getting to the bottom of one of those mindless brawls that happen every day of the week down by the harbour. When my men get there, they're all beating seven bells out of each other. Then they spot uniforms and they close ranks and go on the offensive. Question them and they all lie, contradict each other and muddy the waters to the point that in the end we give up.'

There were four of them smoking in the office, which was already filled with tobacco fumes. It was evening. The divisional head of Le Havre's flying squad, who was officially in charge of the investigation, had a young inspector with him.

Maigret was there in a private capacity. He sat at a table in a corner. He hadn't yet spoken.

'It looks straightforward enough to me,' ventured the young inspector, who was hoping to earn the approval of his chief. 'Theft wasn't the motive for the crime. So it was an act of revenge. On which member of the crew did Captain Fallut come down hardest when they were away at sea?'

But the chief inspector from Le Havre gave a shrug, and the junior inspector turned red and fell silent.

'Still . . .'

'No, no! It's something else. And top of the list is this woman you unearthed for us, Maigret. Did you give the boys in uniform all the information they need to find her? Dammit, I can't for the life of me work out what part she played in all this. The boat was at sea for three months. She wasn't there when it docked, because no one has reported seeing her get off it. The wireless operator is engaged to be married. By all accounts, Captain Fallut didn't seem the kind of man who'd do anything silly. And yet he wrote his will just before he got himself murdered.'

'It would also be interesting to know who exactly went to the trouble of delivering the will here,' sighed Maigret. 'There's also a reporter – he's the one who wears a beige raincoat – who claims in *L'Éclair de Rouen* that the owners of the *Océan* had sent it to sea to do something other than fish for cod.'

'They always say that, every time,' muttered the Fécamp chief inspector.

The conversation languished. There was a long silence during which the spittle in Maigret's pipe could be heard sizzling. He got stiffly to his feet.

'If anyone asked me what the distinctive feature of this case is,' he said, 'I'd say that it has the mark of rage on it. Everything to do with the trawler is acrimonious, tense, overheated. The crew get drunk and fight in the Grand Banks Café. I bring the wireless operator's fiancée to see him, and he could barely conceal his irritation and gave

45

her a pretty cool reception. He almost as good as told her to mind her own business! At Yport, the chief mechanic calls his wife all sorts and treats me like some dog he can kick. And then I come across two people who seem to have the same mark on them: the girl called Adèle, and her boyfriend. They make scenes on the beach, and no sooner do they settle their differences than they disappear together . . .'

'And what do you make of it all?' asked the chief inspector from Le Havre.

'Me? I don't make anything of it. I merely remark that I feel as if I'm going round in circles surrounded by a lot of mad people . . . Anyway, I'll say good night. I'm just an observer here. Besides, my wife is expecting me back at the hotel. You'll let me know, chief inspector, if you locate the Yport woman and the man in the grey car?'

'Of course! Good night!'

Instead of walking through the town, Maigret went via the harbour, hands in pocket, pipe between his teeth. The empty port was a large black rectangle where the only lights that showed were those of the *Océan*, which was still being unloaded.

'. . . the mark of rage!' he muttered to himself.

No one paid attention when he climbed on board. He walked along the deck, with no obvious purpose, he saw a light in a foredeck hatchway. He leaned over it. Warm air blew up into his face, a combined smell of doss-house, canteen and fish market.

He went down the iron ladder and found himself face to face with three men who were eating from mess tins balanced on their knees. For light, there was an oil lamp hung on gimbals. In the middle of their quarters was a cast-iron stove caked with grease.

Along the walls were four tiers of bunks, some still full of straw, the others empty. And boots. And sou'westers hanging on pegs.

Of the three, only Louis had stood up. The other two were the Breton and a black sailor with bare feet.

'Enjoying your dinner?' growled Maigret.

He was answered with grunts.

'Where are your mates?'

'Gone home, haven't they,' said Louis. 'You gotta have nowhere to go and be broke to hang about here when you're not at sea.'

Maigret had to get used to the semi-darkness and especially the smell. He tried to imagine the same space when it was filled by forty men who could not move a muscle without bumping into somebody.

Forty men dropping on to their bunks without taking their boots off, snoring, chewing tobacco, smoking . . .

'Did the captain ever come down here?'

'Never.'

And all the while the throb of the screw, the smell of coal smoke, of soot, of burning hot metal, the pounding of the sea . . .

'Come with me, Louis.'

Out of the corner of his eye, Maigret caught the sailor, full of bravado, making signs to the others behind his back.

But once aloft, on the deck now flooded with shadow, his swagger evaporated.

'What's up?'

'Nothing . . . Listen . . . Suppose the captain died at sea, on the way home. Was there someone who could have got the boat safely back to port?'

'Maybe not. Because the first mate doesn't know how to take a bearing. Still they say that, using the wireless, the wireless operator could always find the ship's position.'

'Did you see much of the wireless operator?'

'Never saw him at all! Don't imagine we walk around like we're doing now. There are general quarters for some, others have separate quarters of their own. You can go for days without budging from your small corner.'

'How about the chief mechanic?'

'Him? Yes. I saw him more or less every day.'

'How did he seem?'

Louis turned evasive.

'How the devil should I know? Look, what are you driving at? I'd like to see how you make out when everything's going wrong, a lad goes overboard, a steam valve blows, the captain's mind is set on anchoring the trawler in a station where there's no fish, a man gets gangrene and the rest of it . . . You'd be effing and blinding nineteen to the dozen! And for the smallest thing you'd take a swing at someone! And to cap it all, when you're told the captain on the bridge is off his rocker . . .'

'Was he?'

'I never asked him. Anyway . . .'

'Anyway what?'

'At the end of the day, what difference will it make? There'll always be someone who'll tell you. Look, it seems there were three of them up top who never went any-where without their revolvers. Three of them spying on each other, all afraid of each other. The captain hardly ever came out of his cabin, where he'd ordered the charts, compass, sextant and the rest to be brought.'

'And it went on like that for three months?'

'Yes. Anything else you want to ask me?'

'No, that's it. You can go . . .'

Louis walked away almost regretfully. He stopped for a moment by the hatch, watching the inspector, who was puffing gently at his pipe.

Cod was still being extracted from the gaping hold in the glare of the acetylene lamps. But Maigret had had enough of trucks, dockers, the quays, the jetties and the lighthouse.

He was standing on a world of plated steel and, half-closing his eyes, he imagined being out on the open sea, in a field of surging swells through which the bows ploughed an endless furrow, hour after hour, day after day, week after week.

'Don't imagine we walk around like we're doing now . . .'

Men below serving the engines. Men in the forward crew quarters. And on the after deck, a handful of God's creatures: the captain, his first mate, the chief mechanic and the wireless operator.

A small binnacle light to see the compass by. Charts spread out.

Three months!

When they'd got back, Captain Fallut had written his will, in which he stated his intention to put an end to his life.

An hour after they'd berthed, he'd been strangled and dumped in the harbour.

And Madame Bernard, his landlady, was left grieving because now there would be no marriage of two ideally suited people. The chief mechanic shouted at his wife. The girl called Adèle defied an unknown man, but ran off with him the moment Maigret held a picture of herself scribbled on in red ink under her nose.

And in his prison cell the wireless operator Le Clinche in a foul temper.

The boat hardly moved. Just a gentle motion, like a chest breathing. One of the three men he'd seen in the foredeck was playing the accordion.

As he turned his head, Maigret made out the shapes of two women on the quayside. Suddenly galvanized, he hurried down the gangway.

'What are you doing here?'

He felt his face burn because he had sounded gruff, but especially because he was aware that he too was being infected by the frenzy which filled all those involved in the case.

'We wanted to see the boat,' said Madame Maigret with disarming self-effacement.

'It's my fault,' said Marie Léonnec. 'I was the one who insisted on . . .'

'All right! That's fine! Have you eaten?'

'It's ten o'clock . . . Have you?'

'Yes, thanks.'

The windows of the Grand Banks Café were more or less the only ones still lit. A few shadowy figures could be made out on the jetty: tourists dutifully out for their evening stroll.

'Have you found out anything?' asked Le Clinche's fiancée.

'Not yet. Or rather, not much.'

'I don't dare ask you a favour.'

'You can always ask.'

'I'd like to see Pierre's cabin. Could I?'

He shrugged and took her there. Madame Maigret refused to walk over the gangway.

Literally a metal box. Wireless equipment. A steel table, a seat and a bunk. Hanging on a wall, a picture of Marie Léonnec in Breton costume. Old shoes on the floor and a pair of trousers on the bed.

The girl inhaled the atmosphere with a mixture of curiosity and delight.

'Yes! But it isn't at all how I'd imagined. His shoes have never been cleaned . . . Oh look! He kept drinking from the same glass without ever washing it . . .'

A strange girl! An amalgam of shyness, delicacy and a good upbringing on the one hand and dynamism and fearlessness on the other. She hesitated.

'And the captain's cabin?'

Maigret smiled faintly, for he realized that deep down she was hoping to make a discovery. He led the way. He even fetched a lantern he found on deck.

'How can they live with this smell?' she sighed.

She looked carefully around her. He saw her become flustered and shy as she said:

'Why has the bed been raised up?'

Maigret stopped drawing on his pipe. She was right. All the crew slept in berths which were more or less part of the architectural structure of the boat. Only the captain had a metal bed.

Under each of its legs a wooden block had been placed.

'You don't think that's strange? It's as if . . .'

'Go on.'

All trace of ill-humour had gone. Maigret saw the girl's pale face lighten as her mind worked and her elation grew.

'It's as if . . . but you'll only laugh at me . . . as if the bed's been propped up so that someone could hide underneath . . . Without those pieces of wood, the bedstead would be much too low, but the way it is now . . .'

And before he could stop her, she lay down flat on the floor regardless of the dirt on the floor and slid under the bed.

'There's enough room!' she said.

'Right. You can come out now.'

'Just a minute, if you don't mind. Pass me that lamp for a minute, inspector.'

She went quiet. He couldn't work out what she was doing. He lost patience.

'Well?'

She reappeared suddenly, her grey suit covered with dust and eyes shining.

'Pull the bed out . . . You'll see.'

Her voice broke. Her hands shook. Maigret yanked the bed away from the wall and looked at the floor.

'I can't see anything . . .'

When she didn't answer he turned and saw that she was crying.

'What did you see? Why are you crying?'

'There . . . Read it.'

He had to bend down and place the lamp against the wall. Then he could make out words scratched on the wood with a sharp object, a pin or a nail.

Gaston – Octave – Pierre – Hen . . .

The last word was unfinished. And yet it did not look as if it had been done in a hurry. Some of the letters must have taken an hour to inscribe. There were flourishes, little strokes, the sort of doodling that's done in an idle moment.

A comic note was struck by two stag's antlers above the name 'Octave'.

The girl was sitting on the edge of the bed, which had been pulled into the middle of the cabin. She was still crying, in silence.

'Very curious!' muttered Maigret. 'I'd like to know if . . .'

At this point, she stood up and said excitedly:

'Of course! That's it! There was a woman here! She was hiding! . . . All the same, men would come looking for her . . . Wasn't Captain Fallut called Octave?'

The inspector had rarely been so taken off guard.

'Don't go jumping to conclusions!' he said, though there was no conviction in his words.

'But it's all written down! . . . The whole story is there! Four men who . . .'

What could he say to calm her down?

'Look, I've a lot of experience, so take it from me. In police matters, you must always wait before making judgements ... Only yesterday, you were telling me that Le Clinche is incapable of killing.'

'Yes,' she sobbed. 'Yes, and I still believe it! Isn't it ...'

She still clung desperately to her hopes.

'His name is Pierre ...'

'I know. So what? One sailor in ten is called Pierre, and there were fifty men on board ... There's also a Gaston ... And a Henry ...'

'So what do you think?'

'Nothing.'

'Are you going to tell the examining magistrate about this? And to think it was me who ...'

'Calm down! We haven't found out anything, except that the bed was raised for one reason or another and that someone has written names on a wall.'

'There was a woman there.'

'Why a woman?'

'But ...'

'Come on. Madame Maigret is waiting for us on the quay.'

'You're right.'

She wiped her tears, meek now, and sniffled.

'I shouldn't have come ... But I thought ... But it's not possible that Pierre ... Listen! I must see him as soon as I can! I'll talk to him, alone ... You can arrange it, can't you?'

Before starting down the gangway, she looked back with eyes full of hate at the dark ship, which was no longer the same to her now that she knew that a woman had been hiding on board.

Madame Maigret watched her, intrigued.

'Come! You mustn't cry! You know everything will all turn out all right.'

'No, it won't,' she said with a despairing shake of her head.

She couldn't speak. She could hardly breathe. She tried to look at the boat one more time. Madame Maigret, who did not understand what was going on, looked inquiringly at her husband.

'Take her back to the hotel. Try and calm her down.'

'Did something happen?'

'Nothing specific. I expect I'll be back quite late.'

He watched them walk away. Marie Léonnec turned round a dozen times, and Madame Maigret had to drag her away like a child.

Maigret thought about going back on board. But he was thirsty. There were still lights on in the Grand Banks Café.

Four sailors were playing cards at a table. Near the counter, a young cadet had his arm round the waist of the serving girl, who giggled from time to time.

The landlord was watching the card game and was offering suggestions.

He greeted Maigret with: 'Hello! You back again?'

He did not look overjoyed to see him. The very opposite. He seemed rather put out.

'Look sharp, Julie! Serve the inspector! Whatever's your poison. It's on me.'

'Thanks. But if it's all the same to you, I'll order like any other customer.'

'I didn't want to get on the wrong side of you . . . I . . .'

Was the day going to end with the mark of rage still on it? One of the sailors muttered something in his Norman dialect which Maigret translated roughly as:

'Watch out, I smell more trouble.'

The inspector looked him in the eye. The man reddened then stammered:

'Clubs trumps!'

'You should have played a spade,' declared Louis for something to say.

5. Adèle and Friend

The phone rang. Léon snatched the receiver, then called Maigret. It was for him.

'Hello?' said a bored voice on the other end of the line. 'Detective Chief Inspector Maigret? It's the duty desk officer at Fécamp police station. I've just phoned your hotel. I was told you might be at the Grand Banks Café. I'm sorry to disturb you, sir. I've been glued to the phone for half an hour. I can't get hold of the chief anywhere. As for the head of the Flying Squad, I'm wondering if he's still actually here in Fécamp . . . Thing is, I've got a couple of odd customers who've just turned up saying they want to make statements, all very urgent, apparently. A man and a woman . . .'

'Did they come in a grey car?'

'Yes, sir. Are they the pair you're looking for?'

Ten minutes later, Maigret was at the police station. All the offices were closed except for the inquiries area, a room divided in two by a counter. Behind it the duty officer was writing. He smoked as he wrote. A man was waiting. He was sitting on a bench, elbows on knees, chin in his hands.

And a woman was walking up and down, beating a tattoo on the floorboards with her high heels

The moment the inspector appeared, she walked right

up to him, and the man got to his feet with a sigh of relief and growled between gritted teeth:

'And not a minute too soon!'

It was indeed the couple from Yport, both a little crosser than during the domestic shouting-match Maigret had sat through.

'Come next door with me.'

Maigret showed them into the office of the chief inspector, sat down in his chair and filled a pipe while he took a good look at the pair.

'Take a seat.'

'No thanks,' said the woman, who was clearly the more highly strung of the two. 'What I've got to say won't take long.'

He now had a frontal view of her, lit by a strong electric light. He did not need to look too hard to situate her type. Her picture with the head removed had been enough.

A good-looking girl, in the popular sense of the expression. A girl with alluring curves, good teeth, an inviting smile and a permanent come-hither look in her eye.

More accurately, a real bitch, a tease, on the make, always ready to create a scandal or burst into gales of loud, vulgar laughter.

Her blouse was pink silk. To it was pinned a large gold brooch as big as a 100-*sou* coin.

'First off, I want to say . . .'

'Excuse me,' interrupted Maigret. 'Please sit down as I've already asked. You will answer my questions.'

She scowled. Her mouth turned ugly.

'Look here! You're forgetting I'm here because I'm prepared to . . .'

Her companion scowled, irritated by her behaviour. They were made for each other. He was every inch the kind who is always seen with girls like her. His appearance was not exactly sinister. He was respectably dressed, though in bad taste. He wore large rings on his fingers and a pearl pin in his tie. Even so, the effect was disturbing. Perhaps because he gave off a sense of existing outside the established social norms.

He was the type to be found at all times of day in bars and brasseries, drinking cheap champagne with working girls and living in third-class hotels.

'You first. Name, address, occupation . . .'

He started to get to his feet.

'Sit down.'

'I just want to say . . .'

'Just say nothing. Name?'

'Gaston Buzier. At present, I'm in the business of selling and renting out houses. I'm based mainly in Le Havre, in the Silver Ring Hotel.'

'Are you a registered property agent?'

'No, but . . .'

'Do you work for an agency?'

'Not exactly . . .'

'That's enough. In a word you dabble . . . What did you do before?'

'I was a commercial traveller for a make of bicycle. I also sold sewing machines out in the sticks.'

'Convictions?'

59

'Don't tell him, Gaston!' the woman broke in. 'You've got a nerve! It was us who came here to . . .'

'Be quiet! Two convictions. One suspended for passing a dud cheque. For the other I got two months for not handing over to the owner an instalment I'd received on a house. Small-time stuff, as you see.'

Even so, he gave the impression that he was used to having to deal with policemen. He stayed relaxed, with something in his eye that suggested he could turn nasty.

'You next,' said Maigret, turning to the woman.

'Adèle Noirhomme. Born in Belleville.'

'On the Vice Squad register?'

'I was put on it five years ago in Strasbourg because some rich cow had it in for me on account of me having snatched her husband off her . . . But ever since . . .'

'. . . you've never been bothered by the police! . . . Fine! . . . Now tell me in what capacity you signed on for a cruise on the *Océan*.'

'First we'd better explain,' the man replied, 'because if we're here, it means we've got nothing to be ashamed of. At Yport, Adèle told me you had a picture of her. She was sure you were going to arrest her. Our first thought was to hop it so we wouldn't get into trouble. Because we both know the score. When we got to Étretat, I saw policemen stopping cars up ahead and I knew they'd go on looking for us. So I decided to come in voluntarily.'

'Now you, lady! I asked what you were doing on board the trawler.'

'Dead simple! I was following my boyfriend.'

'Captain Fallut?'

'Yes, the captain. I'd been with him, so to say, since last November. We met in Le Havre, in a bar. He fell for me. He used to come back to see me two or three times a week. Though from the start I thought he was a bit odd, because he never asked me to do anything. It's true! He was ever so prissy, everything had to be just so! He set me up in a room in a nice little hotel, and I started thinking that if I played my cards right he'd end up marrying me. Sailors don't get rich, but it's steady money, and there's a pension.'

'Did you ever come to Fécamp with him?'

'No. He wouldn't have that. It was him who came to me. He was jealous. He was a decent enough sort who can't have been around much because he was fifty and was as shy with women as a schoolboy. That plus the fact that he'd got me under his skin . . .'

'Just a moment. Were you already the mistress of Gaston Buzier?'

'Sure! But I'd introduced Gaston to Fallut. Said he was my brother.'

'I see. So in short you were both being subsidized by the captain.'

'I was working!' protested Buzier.

'I can see you now, hard at it every Saturday afternoon. And which of you came up with the scheme for sending you to sea on the boat?'

'Fallut. He couldn't bear the thought of leaving me by myself while he was away playing sailors. But he was also scared witless, because the rules about that sort of thing are strict, and he was a stickler for rules. He held out until the very last minute. Then he came and fetched me. The night before he was to set sail, he took me to his cabin. I quite fancied the idea because it made a change. But if I'd known what it was going to be like, I'd have been off like a shot!'

'Buzier didn't try to stop you?'

'He couldn't make up his mind. Do you understand? We couldn't go against what the old fool wanted. He'd promised me he'd retire as soon as he got back after that trip and marry me. But the whole set-up was nothing to write home about! It was no fun being cooped up all day in a cabin that stank of fish! And on top of that, every time anybody came in, I had to hide under the bed! We'd been at sea no time when Fallut start regretting he'd taken me along. I never saw a man have the jitters like him! A dozen times a day he'd check to see if he'd locked the door. If I spoke, he shut me up in case anyone overheard. He was grumpy, on pins . . . Sometimes he'd stare at me for minutes on end as if he was tempted to get rid of me by throwing me overboard.'

Her voice was shrill, and she was waving her arms about.

'Not to mention the fact that he got more and more jealous! He asked me about my past . . . he tried to find out . . . then he'd go three days without talking to me, spying on me like I was his enemy. Then all of a sudden, he'd be madly in love with me again. There were times when I was really scared of him!'

'Which members of the crew saw you when you were on board?'

'It was the fourth night. I felt like a breath of air out on deck. I'd had enough of being locked up. Fallut went out-side and checked to make sure there was no one about. It was as much as he could do to let me walk five steps up and down. He must have gone up on the bridge for a moment, and it was then that the wireless operator showed up and spoke to me . . . He was shy but got worked up. Next day he managed to get into my cabin.'

'Did Fallut see him?'

'I don't think so . . . He didn't mention anything.'

'Did you sleep with Le Clinche?'

She did not answer. Gaston Buzier sneered.

'Admit it!' he barked in a voice full of spite.

'I'm free to do as I please! Especially seeing as how you didn't exactly abstain from female company while I was away! Don't deny it! Are you forgetting the girl from the Villa des Fleurs? And what about that photo I found in your pocket?'

Maigret sat as solemn and impassive as the oracle.

'I asked if you slept with the wireless operator.'

'And I'm telling you to go to blazes!'

She smiled provocatively. Her lips were moist. She knew men desired her. She was counting on the promise of her pouting mouth, her sensuous body.

'The chief mechanic saw you too.'

'What's he been telling you?'

'Nothing. I'll recap. The captain kept you hidden in his cabin. Pierre Le Clinche and the chief mechanic would come to you there, on the quiet. Was Fallut aware of this?'

'No.'

'Although he had his suspicions and prowled round you and never left you alone except when he absolutely had to.'

'How do you know?'

'Did he still talk about marrying you?'

'I don't know.'

In his mind's eye, Maigret saw the trawler, the firemen down in the bunkers, the crew crammed into the foredeck, the wireless room, the captain's cabin aft, with the raised bed.

And the voyage had lasted three months!

All that time three men had prowled round the cabin where this woman was shut away.

'I've done some pretty stupid things, but that . . . !' she exclaimed. 'Hand on heart, if I had to do it again . . . A girl should always be on her guard against shy men who talk about marriage!'

'If you'd listened to me,' said Gaston Buzier.

'You shut your trap! If I'd listened to you, I know what kind of accommodation I'd be in now! I don't want to speak ill of Fallut, because he's dead. But all the same he was cracked. He had peculiar ideas. He'd have thought he'd done something wrong just because he'd broken some rules. And it went from bad to worse. After a week, he never opened his mouth except to go on at me or ask if anybody had been in the cabin. Le Clinche was the one he was most jealous of. He'd say:

'"You'd like that, wouldn't you! A younger man! Say it! Admit that if he came in when I wasn't here you wouldn't turn him away!"

'And he'd laugh so nastily that it hurt.'

'How many times did Le Clinche come to see you?' Maigret asked slowly.

'Oh, all right, the hell with it. Once. On the fourth day. I couldn't even tell you how it happened. After that, it wasn't on the cards, because Fallut kept such a close eye on me.'

'And the mechanic?'

'Never! But he tried! He'd come and look at me through the porthole. When he did that, he looked as white as a sheet . . . What sort of life do you think that was? I was like an animal in a cage. When the sea was rough I was sick, and Fallut didn't even try to look after me. He went for weeks without touching me. Then the urge would come back. He'd kiss me as if he wanted to bite me and held me so tight I thought he was trying to suffocate me.'

Gaston Buzier had lit a cigarette and was now smoking it with a sarcastic expression on his face.

'Please note, inspector, all this had nothing to do with me. While it was going on, I was working.'

'Oh give it a rest, will you?' she said, losing patience.

'What happened when you got back? Did Fallut tell you that he was intending to kill himself?'

'What, him? He didn't say anything. When we got back to port, he hadn't said a single word to me for two weeks. To tell the truth, I don't think he spoke to anyone. He'd stay put for hours with his eyes just staring in front of him. Meantime I'd made up my mind to leave him. I was fed up with it all, wasn't I? I'd have sooner starved to death: I'd never give up my freedom . . . I heard somebody walking along the quayside. Then he came in the cabin and said just a few words:

'"Wait here until I come to fetch you."'

'Spoken like a captain. Didn't he ever speak more . . . fondly?'

'At the finish, no!'

'Go on.'

'I don't know anything else. Or rather, the rest I learned from Gaston. He was there, down at the harbour.'

'Talk!' Maigret ordered the man.

'Like she said, I was down by the harbour. I saw the crew go into the bar. I waited for Adèle. It was dark. Then after a while, the captain came on shore by himself. There were trucks parked nearby. He started walking, and as he did a man jumped him. I don't know exactly what happened but there was a noise like a body falling into the water.'

'Would you recognize the man?'

'No. It was dark, and the trucks stopped me seeing much.'

'Which way did he go when he left?'

'I think he walked along the quay.'

'And you didn't see the wireless operator?'

'I don't know . . . I've no idea what he looks like.'

'And you,' said Maigret, turning to the woman, 'how did you get off the boat?'

'Somebody unlocked the door of the cabin where I was shut in. It was Le Clinche. He said:

'"Go quickly!"'

'Was that all?'

'I tried to ask him what was happening. I heard people

running along the quayside and a boat with a lantern being rowed across the harbour.

'"Get going!" he repeated.

'He pushed me on to the gangway. Everybody was looking the other way. No one paid any attention to me. I had the feeling that something horrible was going on but I preferred to make myself scarce. Gaston was waiting for me a little further along.'

'And what did the two of you do after that?'

'Gaston was as white as a sheet. We went into bars and drank rum. We spent the night at the Railway Inn. The next day all the papers were full of the death of Fallut. So first we took ourselves off to Le Havre, just in case. We didn't want to get mixed up in that business.'

'But that didn't stop her wanting to come back and nose around here,' snapped Gaston. 'I don't know whether it was on account of the wireless operator or . . .'

'Just shut up! That's enough! Of course I was curious about what had happened. So we came back here to Fécamp three times. So that we wouldn't attract attention, we stayed at Yport.'

'And you never saw the chief mechanic again?'

'How do you know about that? One day, in Yport . . . I was scared by the way he looked at me . . . He followed me quite a long way.'

'Why were you arguing earlier this afternoon with Gaston?'

She gave a shrug.

'Because! Look, haven't you got it yet? He thinks I'm in love with Le Clinche, that the wireless operator killed

67

because of me and I don't know what else. He keeps going on and on until I'm sick to death of it. I had my fill of scenes on that damned boat . . .'

'But when I showed you that photo of you, on the hotel terrace . . .'

'Oh very clever! Of course I knew straight off that you were police. I told myself Le Clinche must have talked. I got scared and told Gaston to get us out of there. Only on the way, we thought there was no point because in the end they'd collar us round the next corner. Not to mention the fact that we'd only got two hundred francs between us. What are you going to do with me? . . . You can't send me to jail!'

'Do you think the wireless operator is the killer?'

'How should I know?'

'Do you own a pair of tan-coloured shoes?' Maigret suddenly asked Gaston Buzier.

'I . . . Yes. Why?'

'Oh, nothing. Just asking. Are you absolutely sure you wouldn't be able to recognize the man who killed the captain?'

'All I saw was a man's outline in the dark.'

'Well now, Pierre Le Clinche, who was also there, hidden by the trucks, reckons the murderer was wearing tan shoes.'

Gaston was on his feet like a shot. His eyes were hard, and his lips curled in a snarl.

'He said that? You're sure he said that?'

His anger almost choked him, reduced him to a stammer. He was no longer the same man. He banged the desk with his fist.

'I'm not having this! Take me to him! . . . Where is he? By God! We'll soon see who's lying! Tan-coloured shoes! And that makes me the killer, right? . . . He's the one who took my girl! He's the one who let her off the boat! And he has the nerve to say . . .'

'Calm down.'

He could scarcely breathe. He gasped:

'Did you hear that, Adèle? . . . That's just like all your lover-boys!'

Tears of rage filled both eyes. His teeth chattered.

'This is too much! . . . It wasn't me who . . . ha ha ha . . . this takes the biscuit! It's better than the films! . . . And the minute it comes out that I've got two convictions, he's the one who is believed! So I killed Captain Fallut! . . . Because I was jealous of him, is that it? . . . What else? . . . Oh yes, didn't I kill the wireless operator too?'

He ran one hand feverishly though his hair, which left it in a mess. It also made him look thinner. His eyes had darker rings under them, his complexion was duller.

'If you're going to arrest me, what are you waiting for?'

'Shut up!' snapped Adèle.

But she too had started to panic, though this did not stop her giving Gaston sceptical looks.

Did she have her suspicions? Or was this some sort of play-acting game?

'If you're going to arrest me, do it now . . . But I demand to confront the man . . . Then we'll see!'

Maigret had pressed an electric bell. The station duty officer showed his face warily round the door.

'I want you to keep the gentleman and the lady here

until tomorrow, until we get a ruling from the examining magistrate.'

'You rat!' Adèle yelled at him and she spat on the floor. 'You want to lock me up for telling the truth! . . . Right then, listen to me: every word of what I just told you was made up! . . . I'm not going to sign any statement! . . . That'll put the tin lid on your little scheme! . . . So this is the way . . .'

And turning to Gaston:

'Never mind! . . . They can't touch us! You'll see, when it comes to it it's us who'll have the last laugh . . . Only thing is, a woman who's been on the Vice Squad's books, well, all she's good for is for banging up in the cells . . . Oh by the way, just asking, was it me who killed the captain? . . .'

Maigret left the room without listening to the rest. Outside, he filled his lungs with sea air and knocked the ash out of his pipe. He hadn't gone ten metres when he heard Adèle from inside the police station regaling officers with the choicest items of her vocabulary.

It was now two in the morning. The night was unnaturally calm. It was high tide, and the masts of the fishing boats swayed to and fro above the roofs of the houses.

And over everything the regular murmur, wave after wave, of sea on shingle.

Harsh lights surrounded the *Océan*. It was still being unloaded round the clock, and the dock-hands strained to push the trucks as they filled with cod.

The Grand Banks Café was closed. At the Hôtel de la Plage, the porter, wearing a pair of trousers over his nightshirt, opened the door for the inspector.

The lobby was lit by a single lamp. It was why it took a moment before Maigret made out the figure of a woman in a rattan chair.

It was Marie Léonnec. She was asleep with her head resting on one shoulder.

'I think she's waiting for you,' whispered the porter.

She was pale. And possibly anaemic. There was no colour in her lips, and the dark shadows under her eyes showed just how exhausted she was. She slept with her mouth open, as if she was not getting enough air.

Maigret touched her gently on the shoulder. She gave a start, sat up, looked at him in a daze.

'I must have dropped off . . . Aah!'

'Why aren't you in bed? Didn't my wife see you to your room?'

'Yes. But I came down again. I was very quiet. I wanted to know . . . Tell me . . .'

She was not as pretty as usual because sleep had made her skin clammy. A mosquito bite had left a red spot in the middle of her forehead.

Her dress, which she had probably made herself from hard-wearing serge, was creased.

'Have you found out anything new? No? Listen, I've been thinking a lot. I don't know how to say this . . . Before I see Pierre tomorrow, I want you to talk to him. I want you to say that I know all about that woman, that I don't hate him for it. I'm certain, you see, that he didn't do it. But if I speak to him first, he'll feel awkward. You saw him this morning. He's all on edge, If there was a woman on board, isn't it only natural if he . . .'

But it was too much for her. She burst into tears. She could not stop crying.

'And most of all, nothing must get into the papers. My parents mustn't know. They wouldn't understand. They . . .'

She hiccupped.

'You've got to find the murderer! I think if I could question people . . . I'm sorry, I don't know what I'm saying. You know better than me. Only you don't know Pierre. I'm two years older than him. He's like a little boy really, especially if you accuse him of anything, he is likely to clam up – it's pride – and not say anything. He is very sensitive. He has been humiliated too often.'

Maigret put his hand on her shoulder, slowly, holding back a deep sigh.

Adèle's voice was still going round and round in his head. He saw her again, seductive, desirable in the full bloom of her animal presence, magnificent in her sensuality.

And here was this well-brought-up anaemic girl, who was trying to hold back her tears and smile brightly.

'When you really know him . . .'

But what she would never really know was the dark cabin around which three men had circled for days, for weeks on end, far away, in the middle of the ocean, while other crewmen in the engine room and in the foredeck dimly sensed that a tragedy was unfolding, kept watch on the sea, discussed changes of course, felt increasingly uneasy and talked of the evil eye and madness.

'I'll talk to Le Clinche tomorrow.'

'Can I too?'

'Perhaps. Probably. But now you must get some rest.'

A little later, Madame Maigret, still half-asleep, murmured:

'She's very sweet! Did you know she's already got her trousseau together? All hand-embroidered . . . Find out anything new? You smell of perfume . . .'

No doubt lingering traces of Adèle's overpowering scent which had clung to him. A scent as common as cheap wine in cheap bistros which had, on board the trawler and for months on end, mingled with the rank smell of cod while men prowled round a cabin, as determined and pugnacious as dogs.

'Sleep well!' he said, pulling the blanket up to his chin.

The kiss he placed on the forehead of his drowsy wife was solemn and sincere.

6. *The Three Innocents*

The staging was basic: the setting was the same as for most confrontations of witnesses and accused. This one was taking place in a small office in the jail. Chief Inspector Girard, of the Le Havre police, who was in charge of the investigation, sat in the only chair. Maigret stood with his elbows leaning on the mantelpiece of the black granite fireplace. On the wall were graphs, official notices and a lithograph of the President of the French Republic.

Standing in the full glare of the lamp was Gaston Buzier. He was wearing his tan-coloured shoes.

'Let's have the wireless operator in.'

The door opened. Pierre Le Clinche, who had been given no warning, walked in, brow furrowed, like a man in pain who is expecting to get more of the same treatment. He saw Buzier. But he paid him not the slightest attention and looked all round him, wondering which man he should face.

On the other hand, Adèle's lover looked him up and down, a supercilious smile hanging on his lips.

Le Clinche had a crumpled air. His flesh was grey. He did not try to bluster or conceal his dejection. He was as lost as a sick animal.

'Do you recognize this man here?'

He stared at Buzier, as if searching through his memory.

'No. Who is he?'

'Take a good look at him, from head to foot . . .'

Le Clinche obeyed, and the minute his eyes reached the shoes, he straightened up.

'Well?'

'Yes.'

'Yes what?'

'I understand what you're getting at. The tan shoes . . .'

'So that's it!' Gaston Buzier suddenly burst out. He had not said a word until then but his face was now dark with anger. 'Why don't you tell them again that I'm the one who did your captain in? Go on!'

All eyes were on the wireless operator, who looked at the floor and gestured vaguely with one hand.

'Say it!'

'Perhaps those weren't the shoes.'

'Oh yes!' Gaston crowed, already claiming victory. 'So you're backing down . . .'

'You don't recognize the man who murdered Fallut?'

'I don't know . . . No.'

'You are probably aware that this man is the lover of a certain Adèle, who you most certainly do know. He has already admitted that he was near the trawler at the moment the crime was committed. Also that he was wearing tan-coloured shoes.'

All this time, Buzier was facing him down, bristling with impatience and fury.

'That's right! Make him talk! But he'd better be telling the truth or else I swear I'll . . .'

'Hold your tongue! Well, Le Clinche?'

The young man passed his hand over his brow and winced, literally, with pain.

'I don't know! He can go hang for all I care!'

'But you did see a man wearing tan shoes attack Fallut.'

'I forget.'

'That's what you said when you were first interviewed. That wasn't very long ago. Are you sticking to what you said then?'

'No, that is . . . Look, I saw a man wearing tan shoes. That's all I saw, I don't know if he was the murderer.'

The longer the interview went on, the more confident Gaston Buzier, who also looked rather seedy after a night in the cells, became. He was now shifting his weight from one leg to the other, with one hand in his trouser pocket.

'See? He's backing down! He doesn't dare repeat the lies he told you.'

'Answer me this, Le Clinche. Thus far, we know for certain that there were two men near the trawler at the time when the captain was murdered: you were one, and Buzier the other. You say you didn't kill anybody. Now, after pointing the finger at this man, you seem to be withdrawing the accusation. So was there a third person there? If so, then it is impossible you could not have seen him. So who was it?'

Silence. Pierre Le Clinche continued to stare at the ground.

Maigret, still leaning with elbows propped up on the fireplace, had taken no part in the interrogation, happy to leave it to his colleague and content just to observe the two men.

'I repeat the question: was there a third person on the quay?'

'I don't know,' said the prisoner in a crushed voice.

'Is that a yes?'

A shrug of the shoulder which meant: 'As you wish.'

'Who was it?'

'It was dark.'

'In that case tell me why you said the murderer was wearing tan shoes . . . Wasn't it a way of drawing attention away from the real murderer who was someone you knew?'

The young man clutched his head in both hands.

'I can't take any more!' he groaned.

'Answer me!'

'No! You can do what you like . . .'

'Bring in the next witness.'

The moment the door was open, Adèle walked through it with an exaggerated swagger. She swept the room with one glance to get a sense of what had been going on. Her eye lingered in particular on the wireless operator, whom she seemed shocked to see looking so defeated.

'I assume, Le Clinche, that you recognize this woman, whom Captain Fallut hid in his cabin throughout the entire voyage and with whom you were intimate.'

He looked at her coldly. Yet already Adèle's lips were parting and preparing to frame a captivating smile.

'That's her.'

'To cut a long story short, there were three of you on board, who, in plain language, were sniffing around her: the captain, the chief mechanic and you. You went to bed with her at least once. The chief mechanic got nowhere. Was the captain aware that you had deceived him?'

'He never spoke to me about it.'

'He was very jealous, wasn't he? And it was because he was so jealous that he didn't speak to you for three months?'

'No.'

'No? Was there some other reason?'

Now he was red-faced, not knowing which way to look, talking too fast:

'Well it could have been that. I don't know . . .'

'What else was there between you that might have created hatred or suspicion?'

'I . . . There wasn't anything . . . You're right, he was jealous.'

'What feelings did you have that led you to become Adèle's lover?'

A silence.

'Were you in love with her?'

'No,' he sighed in a small dry voice.

But the woman screeched:

'Thanks a million! Always the gentleman, eh? But that didn't stop you hanging round me until the very last day! Isn't that the truth? And it's also true that you probably had another girl waiting for you on shore!'

Gaston Buzier pretended to be whistling under his breath, with his fingers hooked in the arm-holes of his waistcoat.

'Tell me again, Le Clinche, if, when you went on board after witnessing the death of the captain, Adèle was still locked inside her cabin.'

'Locked in, yes!'

'So she couldn't have killed anyone.'

'No! It wasn't her, I swear!'

Le Clinche was getting ruffled. But Chief Inspector Girard went on remorselessly:

'Buzier states that he didn't kill anybody. But, after accusing him, you withdraw the accusation . . . Another way of looking at it is that the pair of you were in it together.'

'Oh very nice, I must say!' cried Buzier in a burst of brutal contempt. 'When I take up crime, it won't be with a . . . a . . .'

'All right! Both of you could have killed because you were jealous. Both of you had been sleeping with Adèle.'

Buzier said with a sneer:

'Me jealous! Jealous of what?'

'Have any of you anything further to add? You first, Le Clinche.'

'No.'

'Buzier?'

'I wish to state that I am innocent and demand to be released immediately.'

'And you?'

Adèle was putting on fresh lipstick.

'Me . . .' – a thick stroke of lipstick – '. . . I . . .' – a look in her mirror – '. . . I've nothing to say, not a thing . . . All men are skunks! You heard that boy there, the one I'm supposed to have been prepared to do silly things for . . . It's no good looking at me like that, Gaston. Now if you want my opinion, there's things we know nothing about in this business with the boat. The minute you found out a woman had been on board, you thought it explained everything . . . But what if there was something else?'

'Such as?'

'How should I know? I'm not a detective . . .'

She crammed her hair under her red straw toque. Maigret saw Pierre Le Clinche look away.

'The two chief inspectors exchanged glances. Girard said:

'Le Clinche will be returned to his cell. You two will stay in the waiting room . . . I'll let you know whether you are free to go or not in a quarter of an hour.'

The two detectives were left alone. Both looked worried.

'Are you going to ask the magistrate to let them go?' asked Maigret.

'Yes. I think it's the best thing. They may be mixed up in the killing, but there are other things we may be missing . . .'

'Right.'

'Hello, operator? Get me the law courts at Le Havre . . . Hello? . . . Yes, public prosecutor's office please . . .'

A few moments later, while Chief Inspector Girard was talking to the magistrate, there was the sound of a disturbance outside. Maigret ran to see what was happening and saw Le Clinche on the ground, struggling with three uniformed officers.

He was terrifyingly out of control. His eyes were bloodshot and looked wild and staring. Spittle drooled from his mouth. But he was being held down now and couldn't move.

'What happened?'

'We hadn't 'cuffed him, seeing as how he was always so quiet . . . Anyway, as we were moving him down the corridor, he made a grab for the gun in my belt . . . He got it . . . was going to use it to kill himself . . . I stopped him firing it.'

Le Clinche lay on the floor, staring at the ceiling. His teeth were digging into the flesh of his lips, reddening his saliva with blood.

But most disturbing were the tears which streamed down his leaden cheeks.

'Maybe get the doctor . . . ?'

'No! Let him go!' barked Maigret.

When the prisoner was alone on his back on the stone floor:

'On your feet! . . . Look sharp now! . . . Get a move on! . . . And no antics . . . otherwise you'll feel the back of my hand across your face, you miserable little brat!'

The wireless operator did what he was told, unresistingly, fearfully. His whole body trembled with the aftershock. In falling he had dirtied his clothes.

'How does your girlfriend fit into that little display?'

Chief Inspector Girard appeared:

'He agreed,' he said. 'All three are free to go, but they mustn't leave Fécamp . . . What happened here?'

'This moron tried to kill himself! If it's all right with you, I'll look after him.'

The two of them were walking along the quays together. Le Clinche had splashed water over his face. It had not washed the crimson blotches away. His eyes were bright, feverish and his lips too red.

He was wearing an off-the-peg suit with three buttons which he'd done up anyhow, not caring about what he looked like. His tie was badly knotted.

Maigret, hands in pockets, walked grimly and kept muttering as if for his own benefit:

'You've got to understand that I haven't got time to tell you what you should and should not do, except for this: your fiancée is here. She's a good kid, got a lot of grit. She dropped everything and came here all the way from Quimper. She's moving heaven and earth . . . Maybe it wouldn't be such a good idea to dash her hopes . . .'

'Does she know?'

'There's no point in talking to her about that woman.'

Maigret never stopped watching him. They reached the quays. The brightly coloured fishing boats were picked out by the sunshine. The streets nearby were busy.

There were a few moments when Le Clinche seemed to be rediscovering his zest for life, and he looked hopefully at his surroundings with optimism. At others, his eyes hardened, and he glared angrily at people and things.

They had to pass close by the *Océan*, now in the final day of unloading. There were still three trucks parked opposite the trawler.

The inspector spoke casually as he gestured to various points in space.

'You were there . . . Gaston Buzier was here . . . And it was on that spot that the third man strangled the captain.'

Le Clinche breathed deeply, then looked away.

'Only it was dark, and none of you knew who the others were. Anyway, the third man wasn't the chief mechanic or the first mate. They were both with the crew in the Grand Banks Café.'

The Breton, who was outside on deck, spotted the wireless operator, went over to the hatch and leaned his head in. Three sailors came out and looked at Le Clinche.

'Come on,' said Maigret. 'Marie Léonnec is waiting for us.'

'I can't . . .'

'What can't you?'

'Go there! . . . Please, leave me alone! . . . What's it to you if I do kill myself? . . . Anyway, it would be best for all concerned!'

'Is the secret so heavy to bear, Le Clinche?'

No answer.

'And you really can't say anything, is that it? Of course you can. One thing: do you still want Adèle?'

'I hate her!'

'That's not what I asked. I said want, the way you wanted her all the time you were at sea. Just between us men: had you had lots of girls before you met Marie Léonnec?'

'No. Leastways nothing serious.'

'And never deep urges? Wanting a woman so much you could weep?'

'Never!' he sighed and looked away.

'So it started when you were on board ship. There was only one woman, the setting was uncouth, monotonous

. . . Fragrant flesh in a trawler that stank of fish . . . You were about to say something?'

'It's nothing.'

'You forgot all about the girl you were engaged to?'

'That's not the same thing . . .'

Maigret looked him in the eye and was astounded by the change that had just come over it. Suddenly the young man had acquired a determined tilt to his head, his gaze was steady, and his mouth bitter. And yet, for all that, there were traces of nostalgia and fond hopes in his expression.

'Marie Léonnec is a pretty girl,' Maigret went on in pursuit of his line of thought.

'Yes.'

'And much more refined than Adèle. Moreover, she loves you. She is ready to make any sacrifice for . . .'

'Why don't you leave it alone!' said the wireless operator angrily. 'You know very well . . . that . . .'

'. . . that it's something else! That Marie Léonnec is a good, well-brought-up girl, that she will make a model wife and a caring mother but . . . but there'll always be something missing? Isn't that so? Something more elemental, something you discovered on board shut away inside the captain's cabin, when fear caught you by the throat, in the arms of Adèle. Something vulgar, brutal . . . The spirit of adventure! . . . And the desire to bite, to burn your bridges, to kill or die . . .'

Le Clinche stared at him in amazement.

'How did you . . .'

'How do I know? Because everyone has had a sight of the same adventure come his way at least once in his life! . . . We cry hot tears, we shout, we rage! Then, a couple of weeks later, you look at Marie Léonnec and you wonder how on earth you could have fallen for someone like Adèle.'

As he walked, the young man had been keeping his eyes firmly on the glinting water of the harbour. In it were reflected the reds, whites and greens that decorated the taffrails of boats.

'The voyage is over. Adèle has gone. Marie Léonnec is here.'

There was a moment of calm. Maigret went on:

'The ending was dramatic. A man is dead because there was passion on that boat and . . .'

But Le Clinche was again in the grip of wild ideas.

'Stop it! Stop it!' he repeated in a brittle voice. 'No! Surely you can see it's not possible . . .'

He was haggard-eyed. He turned to see the trawler, which, almost empty now, sat high in the water, looming over them.

Then his fears took hold of him once more.

'I swear . . . You've got to let me alone . . .'

'And on board, throughout the entire voyage, the captain was also stretched to breaking point, wasn't he?'

'What do you mean?'

'And the chief mechanic too?'

'No.'

'It wasn't just the two of you. It was fear, Le Clinche, wasn't it?'

'I don't know . . . Please leave me alone!'

'Adèle was in the cabin. Three men were on the prowl.

Yet the captain would not give in to his urges and refused to speak to his woman for days on end. And you, you looked in through the portholes but after just one encounter you never touched her again . . .'

'Stop it!'

'The men down in the bunkers, the crew in the foredeck, they were all talking about the evil eye. The voyage went from bad to worse, lurching from navigational errors to accidents. A ship's boy lost overboard, two men injured, the cod going bad and the mess they made of entering the harbour . . .'

They turned at the end of the quay, and the beach stretched out before them, with its neat breakwater, the hotels, beach-huts and multicoloured chairs dotted over the shingle.

Madame Maigret in a deckchair was picked out by a patch of sunshine. Marie Léonnec, wearing a white hat, was sitting next to her.

Le Clinche followed the direction of Maigret's eyes and stopped suddenly. His temples looked damp.

The inspector went on:

'But it took more than a woman . . . Come on! Your fiancée has seen you.'

And so she had. She stood up, remained motionless for a moment, as if her feelings were too much for her. And then she was running along the breakwater while Madame Maigret put down her needlework and waited.

7. Like a Family

It was one of those situations which crop up spontaneously from which it is difficult to get free. Marie Léonnec, alone in Fécamp, had been placed under the wing of the Maigrets by a friend and had been taking her meals with them.

But now her fiancé was there. All four of them were together on the beach when the hotel bell announced that it was time for lunch.

Pierre Le Clinche hesitated for a moment and looked at the others in embarrassment.

'Come on!' said Maigret, 'we'll get them to lay another place.'

He took his wife's arm as they crossed the breakwater. The young couple followed, not speaking. Or rather, only Marie spoke and did so in a firm voice.

'Any idea what she's telling him?' the inspector asked his wife.

'Yes. She told me a dozen times this morning, to see if I thought it was all right. She's telling him she's not cross with him about anything, *whatever it was that happened*. You see? She's not going to say anything about a woman. She's pretending she doesn't know, but she did say she'd be stressing the words *whatever it was that happened*. Poor girl! She'd go to the ends of the earth for him!'

'Alas!' sighed Maigret.

'What do you mean?'

'Nothing . . . Is this our table?'

Lunch passed off quietly, too quietly. The tables were set very closely together so that speaking in a normal voice was not really possible.

Maigret avoided watching Le Clinche, to put him at his ease, but the wireless operator's attitude gave him cause for concern, and it also worried Marie Léonnec, whose face had a pinched look to it.

Her young man looked grim and depressed. He ate. He drank. He spoke when spoken to. But his thoughts were elsewhere. And more than once, hearing footsteps behind him, he jumped as if he sensed danger.

The bay windows of the dining room were wide open, and through them could be seen the sun-flecked sea. It was hot. Le Clinche had his back to the view and from time to time, with a jerk of the head, would turn round quickly and scour the horizon.

It was left to Madame Maigret to keep the conversation going, mainly by talking to the young woman about nothing in particular, to keep the silence at bay.

Here they were far removed from unpleasant events. The setting was a family hotel. A reassuring clatter of plates and glasses. A half-bottle of Bordeaux on the table next to a bottle of mineral water.

But then the manager made a mistake. He came up as they were finishing dessert and asked:

'Would you like a room to be made up for this gentleman?'

He was looking at Le Clinche: he had spotted a fiancé. And no doubt he took the Maigrets for the girl's parents.

Two or three times the wireless operator made the same gesture as he had that morning during the confrontation. A rapid movement of his hand across his forehead, a very boneless, weary gesture.

'What shall we do now?'

The other guests were getting up and leaving. The group of four were standing on the terrace.

'Shall we sit down for a while?' suggested Madame Maigret.

Their folding chairs were waiting for them, on the shingle. The Maigrets sat down. The two young people remained standing for a moment, uncertain of what they should do.

'I think we'll go for a little walk, shall we?' Marie Léonnec finally brought herself to say with a vague smile meant for Madame Maigret.

The inspector lit his pipe and, once he was alone with his wife, he muttered:

'Tell me: do I really look like the father-in-law!'

'They don't know what to do. Their position is very delicate,' remarked his wife as she watched them go. 'Look at them. They're so awkward. I may be wrong but I think Marie has more backbone than her fiancé.'

He certainly made a sorry sight as he strolled listlessly along, a slight figure who paid no attention to the girl at his side and, you would have sworn even from a distance, did not say anything.

But the girl gave the impression that she was doing her

level best, that she was talking as a way of distracting him, that she was even trying to appear as if she was having a good time.

There were other groups of people on the beach. But Le Clinche was the only man not wearing white trousers. He was wearing a dark suit, which made him look even more pitiful.

'How old is he?' asked Madame Maigret.

Her husband, lying back in his deckchair with eyes half-closed, said:

'Nineteen. Just a boy. I'm very afraid that he'll be easy meat for anybody now.'

'Why? Isn't he innocent?'

'He probably never killed anybody. No. I'd stake my life on it. But all the same, I'm afraid he's had it . . . Just look at him! And look at her!'

'Nonsense. Leave the pair of them alone for a moment and they'll be kissing.'

'Perhaps.'

Maigret was pessimistic.

'She isn't much older than him. She really loves him. She is quite ready to become a model little wife.'

'Why do you think . . .'

'That it won't ever happen? Just an impression. Have you ever looked at photos of people who died young? I've always been struck by the fact that those pictures, which were taken when the subjects were fit and healthy, always have something of the graveyard about them. It's as if those who are doomed to be the victims of some awful experience already have a death sentence written on their faces.'

'And do you think that boy . . .'

'He's a sad case. Always was! He was born poor. He suffered from being poor. He worked like a slave, put his head down, like a man swimming upstream. Then he managed to persuade a nice girl from a higher social class than his to say yes . . . But I don't believe it'll happen. Just look at them. They're groping in the dark. They're trying to believe in happy endings. They want to believe in their star . . .'

Maigret spoke quietly, in a half-whisper, as he stared at the two outlines, which stood out against the sparkling sea.

'Who is officially in charge of the investigation?'

'Girard, a chief inspector at Le Havre. You don't know him. An intelligent man.'

'Does he think he's guilty?'

'No. In any case, he's got nothing solid on him, not even any real circumstantial evidence.'

'What do you think?'

Maigret turned round, as if to get a glimpse of the trawler, though it was hidden from him by a row of houses.

'I think that the voyage was, for two men at least, tragic. Tragic enough that Captain Fallut *couldn't go on living any longer* and the wireless operator *couldn't go back to living his old, normal life.*'

'All because of a woman?'

He did not answer the question directly but went on:

'And the rest of them, the men who had no part in events, all of them including the stokers, were, if they did but know it, deeply marked by it too. They came back angry and scared. For three months, two men and a woman raised the tension around the deck-house in the stern. A few black walls with portholes . . . But it was enough.'

'I've hardly ever seen you get so worked up about a case . . . You said three people were involved. What on earth did they do out there in the middle of the ocean?'

'Yes, what did they do exactly? Something which was serious enough to kill Captain Fallut! And also bad enough to leave those two young people not knowing which way to turn. Look at them out there, trying to find what's left of their dreams in the shingle.'

The young people were coming back, arms swinging, uncertain whether courtesy required them to rejoin the Maigrets or whether it would be more tactful to leave them to themselves.

During their walk, Marie Léonnec had lost much of her vivaciousness. She gave Madame Maigret a dejected look. It was as if all her efforts, all her high spirits had run up against a wall of despair or inertia.

It was Madame Maigret's custom to take some light refreshment of an afternoon. So at around four o'clock, all four of them sat down on the hotel terrace under the striped umbrellas, which exuded the customary festive air.

Hot chocolate steamed in two cups. Maigret had ordered a beer and Le Clinche a brandy and soda.

They talked about Jorissen, the teacher from Quimper who had written to Maigret on behalf of the wireless operator and had brought Marie Léonnec with him. They said the usual things:

'You won't find a better man anywhere . . .'

They embroidered on this theme, not out of conviction, but because they had to say something. Suddenly, Maigret blinked, then focused on a couple now walking towards them along the breakwater.

It was Adèle and Gaston Buzier. He slouched, hands in pockets, his boater tilted on the back of his head, seemingly unconcerned, while she was as animated and as eye-catching as ever.

'As long as she doesn't spot us . . . !' the inspector thought.

But at that very moment, Adèle's eye caught his. She stopped and said something to her companion, who tried to dissuade her.

Too late! She was already crossing the road. She looked around at all the tables in turn, chose the one nearest to the Maigrets, then sat down so that she was facing Marie Léonnec.

Her boyfriend followed with a shrug, touched the brim of his boater as he passed in front of the inspector and sat astride a chair.

'What are you having?'

'Not hot chocolate, that's for sure. A kümmel.'

What was that if not a declaration of war? When she mentioned chocolate, she was staring at Marie Léonnec's cup. Maigret saw the girl flinch.

She had never seen Adèle. But surely the penny had dropped? She glanced across at Le Clinche, who looked away.

Madame Maigret's foot nudged her husband's twice.

'What say the four of us walk over to the Casino.'

She too had worked it out. But no one answered. Only Adèle at the next table said anything.

'It's so hot!' she sighed. 'Take my jacket, Gaston.'

She removed her suit jacket and was revealed in pink silk, opulently sensual and bare-armed. She did not take her eyes off the girl for an instant.

'Do you like grey? Don't you think they should ban people from wearing miserable colours on the beach?'

It was so obvious. Marie Léonnec was wearing grey. But Adèle was demonstrating her intention to go on the attack, by any means and without wasting any time.

'Waiter! Shift yourself! I can't wait all day.'

Her voice was shrill. And it sounded as if she was deliberately exaggerating its coarseness.

Gaston Buzier scented danger. He knew Adèle of old. He muttered a few words to her. But she replied in a very loud voice:

'So what? They can't stop anyone sitting on this terrace. It's a free country!'

Madame Maigret was the only one with her back to her. Maigret and the wireless operator sat sideways on but Marie Léonnec faced her directly.

'We're all as good as everybody else, isn't that right? Only there's some people who trail round after you when you're too busy to see them and then won't give you the time of day when they're in company.'

And she laughed. Such an unpleasant laugh! She stared at the girl, whose face flushed bright red.

'Waiter! What do I owe you?' asked Buzier, who was anxious to put a stop to this.

'We've got plenty of time! Same again, waiter. And bring me some peanuts.'

'We don't have any.'

'Well go and get some! That's what you're paid for, isn't it?'

There were people at two other tables. They all stared at the new couple, who could not go unnoticed. Maigret began to worry. He wanted of course to put an end to a scene which might turn nasty.

On the other hand, the wireless operator was trapped opposite him: he could see him sit there and sweat.

It was fascinating, like being present at a dissection. Le Clinche did not move a muscle. He was not facing the woman, but he must surely have been able to see her, however vaguely, on his left, at the very least to make out the pink cloud of her blouse.

His eyes, grey and lacklustre, were fixed and staring. One hand lay on the table and was closing slowly, as slowly as the tentacles of some undersea creature.

There was no telling yet how it would all turn out. Would he get up and run away? Would he turn on the woman who talked and talked? Would he . . . ?

No. He did none of those things. What he did was quite different and a hundred times more unnerving. It was not just his hand that was closing, but his whole being. He was shrivelling, shrinking into his shell.

His eyes steadily turned as grey as his face.

He did not move. Was he still breathing? Not a tremor. Not a twitch. But his stillness, which grew more and more complete, was mesmerizing.

'. . . puts me in mind with another of my gentleman friends, married he was, with three kids . . .'

Marie Léonnec, on the other hand, was breathing quickly. She gulped down her chocolate to hide her confusion.

'. . . now he was the most passionate man on the planet. Sometimes, I refused to let him in and he'd stop outside on the landing and sob, until the neighbours worked up a right old head of steam! "Adèle my sweety pie, my pet, my own . . ." All the usual lovey-dovey stuff. Anyway, one Sunday I met him out walking with his wife and kiddies. I heard his wife ask him:

'"Who's that woman?"

'And all pompous, he says to her:

'"Obviously a floozie. You can tell from the ridiculous way she's dressed."'

And she laughed, playing to the crowd. She looked at the faces around her to see what effect her behaviour was having.

'Some people are that slow on the uptake you can't get a rise out of them.'

Again Gaston Buzier said something to her quietly in an attempt to shut her up.

'What's the matter? Not turning chicken are you? I pay for my drinks, don't I? I'm not doing anybody any harm! So nobody's got any right to tell me what to do . . . Waiter, where are those peanuts? And bring another kümmel!'

'Maybe we should leave,' said Madame Maigret.

It was too late. Adèle was on the rampage. It was clear

that if they tried to leave, she would do anything to cause a scene, whatever the cost.

Marie Léonnec was staring at the table. Her ears were red, her eyes unnaturally bright, and her mouth hung open in distress.

Le Clinche had shut his eyes. And he went on sitting there, unseeing, with a fixed expression on his face. His hand still lay lifelessly on the table.

Maigret had never had an opportunity like this to scrutinize him. His face was both very young and very old, as is often the case with adolescents who have had difficult childhoods.

Le Clinche was tall, taller than average, but his shoulders were not yet those of a man.

His skin, which he had not looked after, was dotted with freckles. He had not shaved that morning, and there were faint blond shadows around his chin and on his cheeks.

He was not handsome. He could not have laughed very often in his life. On the contrary, he had burned large quantities of midnight oil, reading too much, writing too much, in unheated rooms, in his ocean-tossed cabin, by the light of dim lamps.

'I'll tell you what really makes me sick. It's seeing people putting on airs who're really no better than us.'

Adèle was losing patience. She was ready to try anything to get what she wanted.

'All these proper young ladies, for instance. They pretend to be lily-white hens but they'll run after a man the way no self-respecting trollop would dare to.'

The hotel owner stood by the entrance, surveying his

guests as if trying to decide whether or not he should intervene.

Maigret now had eyes only for Le Clinche, in close-up. His head had dropped a little. His eyes had not opened.

But tears squeezed out one by one from under his clamped eyelids, oozed between the eyelashes, hesitated and then snaked down his cheeks.

It wasn't the first time the inspector had seen a man cry. But it was the first time he had been so affected by the sight. Perhaps it was the silence, the stillness of his whole body.

The only signs of life it gave were those rolling, liquid pearls. The rest was dead.

Marie Léonnec had seen nothing of all this. Adèle was still talking.

Then, a split second later, Maigret *knew*. The hand which lay on the table had just imperceptibly opened. The other was out of sight, in a pocket.

The lids rose no more than a millimetre. It was enough to allow an eye-glance to filter through. That glance settled on Marie.

As the inspector was getting to his feet, there was a gunshot. Everyone reacted in a confused pandemonium of screams and overturned chairs.

At first, Le Clinche did not move. Then he started to lean imperceptibly to his left. His mouth opened, and from it came a faint groan.

Marie Léonnec, who had difficulty understanding what had happened, since no one had seen a gun, flung herself

98

on him, grabbed him by the knees and his right hand and turned in panic:

'Inspector! . . . What . . . ?'

Only Maigret had worked out what had happened. Le Clinche had had a revolver in his pocket, a weapon he had found God knows where, for he hadn't had one that morning when he was released from his cell. And he'd fired from his pocket. He'd been gripping the butt all the interminable time Adèle had been talking, while he kept his eyes shut and waited and maybe hesitated.

The bullet had caught him in the abdomen or the side. His jacket was scorched, cut to ribbons at hip level.

'Get a doctor! Ring for the police!' someone somewhere was shouting.

A doctor appeared. He was wearing swimming trunks. He'd been on the beach hardly a hundred metres from the hotel.

Hands had reached out and held Le Clinche up just as he began to fall. He was carried into the hotel dining room. Marie, utterly distraught, followed the stretcher inside.

Maigret had not had time to worry about Adèle or her boyfriend. As he entered the bar, he suddenly saw her. She looked deathly pale and was emptying a large glass, which rattled against her teeth.

She had helped herself. The bottle was still in her hand. She filled the glass a second time.

The inspector paid her no further attention, but retained the image of that white face above the pink blouse and particularly the sound of her teeth chattering against the glass.

He could not see Gaston Buzier anywhere. The dining-room door was about to be closed.

'Move along, please,' the hotel-owner was telling guests. 'Keep calm! The doctor has asked us to keep the noise down.'

Maigret pushed the door open. He found the doctor kneeling and Madame Maigret restraining the frantic Marie, who was trying desperately to rush to the wounded man's side.

'Police!' the inspector muttered to the doctor.

'Can't you get those women out of here? I'm going to have to undress him and . . .'

'Right.'

'I'll need a couple of men to help me. I assume someone has already phoned for an ambulance?'

He was still wearing his trunks.

'Is it serious?'

'I can't tell you anything until I've probed the wound. You do of course understand . . .'

Yes! Maigret understood all too well when he saw the appalling, lacerated mess, a coalescence of flesh and fabric.

The tables had been laid for dinner. Madame Maigret took Marie Léonnec outside. A young man in white trousers asked shyly:

'If you'll allow me, I could help . . . I'm studying pharmacy.'

A burst of fierce red sunlight slanted through a window and was so blindingly bright that Maigret closed the Venetian blind.

'Will you take his legs?'

He recalled the words he had said to his wife that afternoon as he lounged in his folding chair watching the gangling figure move across the beach with the smaller and livelier outline of Marie Léonnec at his side:

'Easy meat.'

Captain Fallut had died as soon as he had docked. Pierre Le Clinche had fought long and hard, perhaps had even still been fighting as he sat eyes closed, one hand on the table, the other in his pocket, while Adèle went on talking, endlessly talking and playing to the gallery.

8. *The Drunken Sailor*

It was a little before midnight when Maigret left the hospital. He had waited to see the stretcher being wheeled out of the operating theatre. On it lay the prone figure of a tall man swathed in white.

The surgeon was washing his hands. A nurse was putting the instruments away.

'We'll do our best to save him,' he said in reply to the inspector. 'His intestine is perforated in seven places. You could say it's a very, very nasty wound. But we've tidied him up.'

He gestured to receptacles full of blood, cotton-wool and disinfectant.

'Believe me, it took a lot of damned hard work!'

They were all in high good humour, surgeons, assistant-surgeons and theatre nurses. They had been brought a patient as near to death's door as he could be, bloodstained, abdomen not only gaping but scorched too, with scraps of clothing embedded in his flesh.

And now an ultra-clean body had just been carried out on a trolley. And the abdomen had been carefully stitched up.

The rest would be for later. Maybe Le Clinche would regain consciousness, maybe not. The hospital did not even try to find out who he was.

'Does he really have a chance of pulling through?'

'Why not? We used to see worse than that during the War.'

Maigret had phoned the Hôtel de la Plage at once, to set Marie Léonnec's mind at rest. Now he set out to walk back by himself. The doors of the hospital closed behind him with the smooth sound of well-oiled hinges. It was dark. The street of small middle-class houses was deserted.

He had only gone a few metres when a figure stepped away from the wall and the light of a street lamp illuminated the face of Adèle. In a mean voice she asked:

'Is he dead?'

She must have been waiting for hours. Her features were drawn, and the kiss-curls at her temples had lost their shape.

'Not yet,' replied Maigret in the same tone of voice.

'Will he die?'

'Maybe, maybe not.'

'Do you think I did it on purpose?'

'I don't think anything.'

'Because it's not true!'

The inspector continued on his way. She followed him and to do so she had to walk very quickly.

'Basically, it was his own fault, you must see that.'

Maigret pretended he wasn't even listening. But she was stubborn and persisted:

'You know very well what I mean. On board he nearly got to the point of asking me to marry him. Then once we'd docked . . .'

She would not give up. She seemed driven by an over-mastering need to talk.

'If you think I'm a bad woman, it's because you don't know me. Only, there are times . . . Look, inspector, you've got to tell me the truth. I know what a bullet can do, especially in the belly from point-blank range. They performed a laparotomy on him, right?'

She gave the impression that she was no stranger to hospitals, that she had heard how doctors talked and knew people who'd been shot more than once.

'Was the operation a success? . . . I believe it depends on what the patient has been eating before . . .'

Her distress was not acute. More a raw, stubborn refusal to take no for an answer.

'Aren't you going to say? But there, you know, don't you, why I sounded off like that this afternoon. Gaston is a cheap crook. I never loved him. But the other one . . .'

'He may live,' said Maigret carefully, looking the girl straight in the eyes. 'But if what happened on the *Océan* is not cleared up, it won't do him much good.'

He paused, expecting her to say something, to have a reaction. She dropped her eyes.

'Of course, you think that I know everything . . . From the moment both men were my lovers . . . But I swear . . . ! No, you don't know what sort of man Captain Fallut was, so you'll never understand . . . He was in love with me, it's true. He used to come to Le Havre to see me. And falling, I mean really falling, for a woman at his age turned his brain . . . But that did not stop him being pernickety about everything, very controlled, very faddy about wanting everything just so . . . I still can't work out why he ever agreed to let me hide on board . . . But what I do know is the minute we were out on the open sea he regretted it and because he regretted it he began to hate me . . . His character changed just like that.'

'But the wireless operator hadn't spotted you yet?'

'No. That didn't happen until the fourth night, like I told you . . .'

'Are you quite sure that Fallut was already in a strange mood before then?'

'Maybe not quite as strange. But afterwards there were days when it all got weird, and I wondered if he wasn't actually mad.'

'And you had no idea about what the reason for the change might have been?'

'No. I thought about it. Sometimes I told myself there had to be some funny business going on between him and the wireless operator. I even thought they were involved in smuggling . . . Ah, you won't ever get me to go anywhere near a fishing boat again! Can you believe that it went on for three months? And then for it to end like that! One is murdered as soon as he steps ashore and the other who . . . It is true, isn't it, that he's not dead?'

They had reached the quays, and the young woman seemed reluctant to go any further.

'Where is Gaston Buzier?'

'Back at the hotel. He knows it's not the moment to rub me up the wrong way, that I'd dump him if he says one word out of place.'

'Are you going back to him now?'

She gave a shrug, a gesture which signified: 'Why not?'

And then there was a glimpse of her flirtatious self. Just as she was taking her leave of Maigret, she murmured with an awkward smile:

'Thank you so much, inspector. You've been ever so kind . . . I . . .'

But she didn't dare say the rest. It was an invitation. A promise.

'All right, all right!' he growled and walked on.

He pushed open the door of the Grand Banks Café.

Just as he reached for the latch, he clearly heard a hubbub coming from inside the bar, like a dozen men's voices all talking at once. The moment the door opened, complete silence fell with brutal abruptness. Yet there were more than ten men there, in two or three groups, who must have been calling to each other from one table to the next.

The landlord stepped forward to meet Maigret and shook his hand, though not without a certain unease of manner.

'Is it true what they're saying? That Le Clinche shot himself?'

His customers toyed with their drinks in a show of indifference. Present were Louis, the black sailor, the chief mechanic from the trawler and a few others besides whom Maigret had finally got to know by sight.

'Quite true,' he said.

He observed that the chief mechanic, looking suddenly very shifty, kept fidgeting on the oil-cloth of the bench seat.

'Some voyage!' muttered someone in a corner in a pronounced Norman accent.

The words probably were a fair expression of the general opinion, for many heads dropped, a fist was brought down on a marble tabletop while one voice echoed the sentiment:

'Yes! A voyage of the damned!'

But Léon gave a cough to remind his customers to watch what they said and with a nod to them motioned towards a sailor in a red jerkin, who was drinking alone in a corner.

Maigret sat down near the counter and ordered a brandy and soda.

No one was talking now. Every man there was trying to look calm and unruffled. Léon, a practised master of ceremonies, called out to the group sitting around the largest table:

'Want me to bring the dominoes?'

It was a way of breaking the silence, of occupying hands. The black-backed dominoes were shuffled on the marble tabletop. The landlord sat down next to the inspector.

'I shut them up,' he said quietly, 'because the fellow in the far corner, to your left, by the window, is the father of the boy . . . You know who I mean?'

'What boy?'

'The ship's boy, Jean-Marie, the one who fell overboard on their third day out.'

The man had his head on one side and was listening. If he hadn't heard the words, he had certainly understood that they concerned him. He called to the serving girl to refill his glass and downed it in one, with a shudder of disgust.

He was already drunk. He had bulging light-blue eyes which were now more sea-green. A quid of tobacco raised a lump in his cheek.

'Does he go out on the Grand Banks boats too?'

'He used to. But now that he's got seven kids, he goes out after herring in winter, because the periods away are shorter: a month to start with and then for increasingly shorter spells as the fish go south.'

'And in summer?'

'He fishes for himself, lays dragnets, lobster pots . . .'

The man was sitting on the same bench-seat as Maigret, at the far end of it. But the inspector had a good view of him in a mirror.

He was short, with wide shoulders. He was a typical northern sailor, squat, fleshy, with no neck, pink skin and fair hair. Like most fishermen, his hands were covered with scars of old ulcers.

'Does he usually drink this much?'

'They're all hard drinkers. But he's been really knocking it back since his boy died. Seeing the *Océan* again hit him hard.'

The man was now staring at them, openly insolent.

'What you after, then?' he spluttered at Maigret.

'Nothing at all.'

All the mariners followed the scene without interrupting their game of dominoes.

'Because you'd better out with it . . . A man's not entitled to have a drink, is that it?'

'Not at all!'

'Go on, say it, say I'm not entitled to have a sup or two,' he repeated with the obstinacy of a drunk.

The inspector's eye picked out the black armband he wore on one sleeve of his red jerkin.

'So what you up to, then, sneaking around here, the pair of you, talking about me?'

Léon shook his head, advising Maigret not to reply, and went over to his customer.

'Easy now! Don't go kicking up a fuss, Canut. The inspector's not talking about you but about the lad who shot himself.'

'Serve him right! Is he dead?'

'No. Maybe they can save him.'

'Too bad! I wish they'd all die!'

The words had an immediate impact. All heads turned to stare at Canut, who felt the urge to shout it ever louder:

'That's right! The whole lot of you!'

Léon was worried. He looked imploringly at everyone there, adding a gesture of helplessness in Maigret's direction.

'Go home. Go to bed. Your wife will be waiting up . . .'

'Don't give a damn!'

'In the morning, you won't feel like going out to clear your nets.'

The drunk sniggered. Louis took the opportunity to call to Julie:

'How much does it come to?'

'Both rounds?'

'Yes. Put it on the slate. Tomorrow I'll get my advance pay before I sail.'

He got to his feet. The Breton automatically followed his lead, as if he were his shadow. He tipped his cap. Then he did it again for Maigret's particular benefit.

'Bunch of chicken-hearts!' muttered the drunk as the two men walked past him. 'Cowards, the whole lot of them!'

The Breton clenched his fists and was about to say something. But Louis dragged him away.

'Go home to bed,' Léon repeated. 'Anyway, it's closing time.'

'I'll go when everybody else goes. My money's as good as the next man's, right?'

He looked around for Maigret. It was as if he was ready to start an argument.

'It's like the big fella there . . . What's he trying to ferret out?'

He was referring to the inspector. Léon was on tenter-hooks. The last customers lingered, sure that something was about to happen.

'Second thoughts, I think I'd rather go home. What do I owe you?'

He fumbled beneath his jerkin and produced a leather wallet, threw a few greasy notes on the table, stood up, swayed and staggered to the door, which he had difficulty opening.

He kept muttering indistinctly what might have been insults or threats. Once outside, he pressed his face to the window for a last look at Maigret, flattening his nose against the steamed-up glass.

'It hit him real hard,' sighed Léon, returning to his seat. 'He had just the one son. All his other kids are girls. Which is to say they don't count.'

'What are they saying here?' asked Maigret.

'About the wireless operator? They don't know anything. So they make things up. Fanciful tales . . .'

'Such as?'

'Oh, I don't know. They're always on about the *evil eye* . . .'

Maigret sensed that there was a keen eye watching him. It belonged to the chief mechanic, who was sitting at the table opposite.

'Has your wife stopped being jealous?' the inspector asked.

'Given that we sail in the morning, I'd like to see her try to keep me stuck in Yport!'

'Is the *Océan* leaving tomorrow?'

'With the tide, yes. If you think the owners intend to let her fester in the harbour . . .'

'Have they found a new captain?'

'Some retired master or other who hasn't been at sea for eight years. And on top of that, he was then skipper of a three-masted barque! It'll be no fun!'

'And the wireless operator?'

'Some kid they've got straight out of college . . . Some big technical school, they said it was.'

'And is the first mate coming back?'

'They recalled him. Sent him a cable. He'll be here in the morning.'

'And the crew?'

'The usual story. They take whatever's hanging around the docks. It always works, doesn't it?'

'Have they found a ship's boy?'

The chief mechanic looked at him sharply.

'Yes,' he said curtly.

'Glad to be off?'

No reply. The chief mechanic ordered another grog. Léon, keeping his voice low, said:

'We've just had news of the *Pacific*, which was due back this week. She's a sister ship of the *Océan*. She sank in less than three minutes after splitting her seams on a rock. All hands lost. I've got the first mate's wife staying upstairs. She came from Rouen to meet her husband. She spends every day down by the harbour mouth. She doesn't know yet. The Company is waiting for confirmation before breaking the news.'

'It's the design of those boats,' growled the chief mechanic, who had overheard.

The black sailor yawned and rubbed his eyes but was not thinking of leaving just yet. The abandoned dominoes formed a complicated pattern on the grey rectangle of the tabletop.

'So in a word,' Maigret said slowly, 'no one has any idea why the wireless operator tried to kill himself?'

His words met with an obstinate silence. Did all the men there know why? Was this the freemasonry of seamen taken to an extreme, closing ranks against landlubbers who poked their noses into their business?

'What do I owe you, Julie?' asked Maigret.

He stood up, paid, headed wearily to the door. Ten

pairs of eyes followed him. He turned but saw only faces that were blank or resentful. Even Léon, for all his bar-keeper's chumminess, stood shoulder to shoulder with his customers.

It was low tide. All that could be seen of the trawler was the funnel and the derricks. The trucks had all gone. The quay was deserted.

A fishing boat, with its white light swinging at the end of its mast, was slowly moving away towards the jetties, and the sound of two men talking could be heard.

Maigret filled one last pipe, looked across the town and the towers of the Palais de la Bénédictine, at the foot of which were walls which were part of the hospital.

The windows of the Grand Banks Café punctuated the quay with two rectangles of light.

The sea was calm. There was a faint murmur of water lapping the shingle and the wooden piles of the jetties.

The inspector stood on the edge of the quay. Thick hawsers, the ones holding the *Océan* fast, were coiled round bronze bollards.

He leaned over. Men were battening down the hatches over the holds in which salt had been stowed earlier that day. One of them was very young, younger than Le Clinche. He was wearing a suit and, leaning against the wireless room, was watching the sailors as they worked.

It could only be the replacement for the wireless oper-ator who not long since had put a bullet in his own belly. He was smoking a cigarette, taking shallow, nervous pulls on it.

He'd come straight from Paris, fresh out of the National

Technical School. He was apprehensive. Perhaps he dreamed of adventure.

Maigret could not tear himself away. He was rooted there by a feeling that the mystery was close, within his grasp, that he had to make just one last effort.

Suddenly, he turned, sensing a strange presence behind him. In the dark, he made out a red jerkin and a black armband.

The man had not seen him, or at least was not paying him any attention. He was walking along the lip of the quayside, and it was a miracle that in the state he was in that he did not go over the edge.

The inspector now had only a rear view of him. He had a feeling that the drunk, overcome by dizziness, was about to fall down on to the deck of the trawler.

But no. He was talking to himself. He laughed derisively. He brandished a fist.

Then he spat, once, twice, three times on the boat below. He spat to express his total and utter disgust.

After which, doubtless having relieved his feelings, he wandered off, not in the direction of his house, which was in the fishermen's quarter, but towards the lower end of town, where there was a bar still with its lights on.

9. Two Men on Deck

From the cliff side of the town came a silvery chime: it was the clock of the Palais de la Bénédictine, striking one.

Maigret, his hands clasped behind him, was walking back to the Hôtel de la Plage. But the further he went the slower he walked until he finally came to a complete stop halfway along the quay.

In front of him was his hotel, his room and his bed, a welcoming, comforting combination.

Behind him . . . He turned his head. He saw the trawler's funnel, from which smoke was gently rising, for the boilers had just been lit. Fécamp was asleep. There was a wide splash of moonlight in the middle of the harbour. The wind was rising, blowing in off the sea, raw and almost freezing, like the breath of the ocean itself.

Maigret turned back wearily, reluctantly. Again he stepped over the hawsers coiled round the bollards, then stood on the side of the quay, staring down at the *Océan*.

His eyes were small, his mouth threatening, his hands were bunched into fists deep in his pockets.

Here was Maigret in solitary mood, disgruntled, withdrawn, when he digs his heels in defiantly and is not afraid of making a fool of himself.

It was low tide. The deck of the trawler was four or five

metres below the level of the quay. But a plank had been laid between the quayside and the bridge. It was thin and narrow.

The sound of the surf was growing louder. The tide must be on the turn. Pallid waves ate imperceptibly into the shingle of the beach.

Maigret stepped on to the plank, which bent into the arc of a circle when he reached the middle. His soles squealed when he reached the iron bridge. But he did not go any further. He sat down on the seat of the officer of the watch, behind the wheel and the compass, from which dangled Captain Fallut's thick sea mittens.

Maigret settled in the way grim dogs crouch stubbornly by the mouth of a burrow where they have got a scent of something.

Jorissen's letter, his friendship with Le Clinche, all the steps taken by Marie Léonnec were no longer the issue. It was now personal.

He had formed a picture of Captain Fallut. He had met the wireless operator, Adèle and the chief mechanic. He had gone to considerable lengths to get a sense of the whole way of life on board the trawler.

But it was not enough. Something was eluding him. He felt he understood everything except, crucially, what was at the heart of the case.

Fécamp was asleep. On board, the sailors were in their bunks. The inspector slumped heavily in the seat of the officer of the watch, round-shouldered, legs slightly apart, his elbows on his knees.

His eye settled on random details: the gloves, for

instance, huge, misshapen, which Fallut would have worn during his spells on the bridge and had left hanging there.

And half turning, he looked back over the afterdeck. Ahead were the full sweep of the deck, the foredeck and, very near, the wireless room.

The sound of water lapping. A barely perceptible surge as the steam began to stir. Now that the furnace had been lit and water filled the boilers, the boat felt more alive than it had in the last few days.

And wasn't Louis asleep below, next to the bunkers full of coal?

To the right was the lighthouse. At the end of one jetty, a green light; a red light at the head of the next.

And the sea: a great black hole emitting a strong, heavy smell.

There was no conscious effort of the mind involved, not in the strict sense. Maigret let his eye roam slowly, sluggishly, seeking to bring his surroundings to life, to acquire a feel for them. Gradually he slipped into something akin to a state of trance.

'It was a night like this, but colder, because spring had scarcely begun . . .'

The trawler, tied up at the same berth. A thin spiral of smoke rising from the funnel.

A few sleeping men.

Pierre Le Clinche, who had dined at Quimper in his fiancée's house. Family atmosphere. Marie Léonnec had doubtless shown him to the door, so that they could kiss unobserved.

And he had travelled all night, third class. He would

return in three months. He would see her again. Then another voyage and after that, when it was winter, around Christmas time, they would marry.

He had not slept. His sea-chest was on the rack. It contained provisions made for him by his mother.

At the same time, Captain Fallut was leaving the small house in Rue d'Étretat, where Madame Bernard was asleep.

Captain Fallut was probably uneasy and very troubled, racked in advance by guilt. Was it not tacitly agreed that one day he would marry his landlady?

Yet all winter he had been going to Le Havre, sometimes three times a week, to see a woman. A woman he dared not show his face with in Fécamp. A woman he was keeping as his mistress. A woman who was young, attractive, desirable, but whose vulgarity gave her an aura of danger.

A respectable man, of regular, fastidious habits. A model of probity, held up as an example by his employers, whose sea-logs were masterpieces of detailed record-keeping.

And now he was making his way through the sleeping streets to the station where Adèle was due to arrive.

Perhaps he was still hesitating?

But three months! Would he find her waiting for him when he got back? Wasn't she too alive, too eager for life not to deceive him?

She was a very different kind of woman from Madame Bernard. She did not spend her time keeping her house tidy, polishing brasses and floors, making plans for the future.

Absolutely not! She was a woman, a woman whose

image was fixed on his retina in ways that brought a flush to his cheek and quickened his breath.

Then she was there! She laughed with that tantalizing laugh which was almost as sensual as her inviting body. She thought it would be fun to sail away, to be hidden on board, to have a great adventure!

But should he not tell her that the adventure would not be much fun? That being at sea cooped up in a locked cabin would be an ordeal?

He vowed that he would. But he didn't dare. When she was there, when her breasts heaved as she laughed, he was incapable of saying anything sensible.

'Are you going to smuggle me on board tonight?'

They walked on. In the bars and the Grand Banks Café, members of the crew went on the spree with the advance on their wages they'd been paid that afternoon.

And Captain Fallut, short, smartly turned out, grew paler the nearer he got to the harbour, to his boat. Now he could see the funnel. His throat was dry. Perhaps there was still time?

But Adèle was hanging on his arm. He could feel her leaning against him, warm and trembling with excitement.

Maigret, facing the quayside which was now deserted, imagined the two of them.

'Is that your ship? It smells bad. Have we got to go across on this plank?'

They walked over the gangway. Captain Fallut was nervous and told her to not to make a noise.

'Is this the wheel for driving the ship?'

'Sh!'

They went down the iron ladder. They were on the deck. They went into the captain's cabin. The door closed behind them.

'Yes! That's how it was!' muttered Maigret. 'There they are now, the pair of them. It's the first night on board . . .'

He wished he could fling back the curtain of night, reveal the pallid sky of first light and make out the figures of the crew staggering, slowed by alcohol, as they made their way back to the boat.

The chief mechanic arrived from Yport by the first morning train. The first mate was on the way from Paris and Le Clinche from Quimper.

The men tumbled on to the deck, argued in the foredeck about bunks, laughed, changed their clothes and re-emerged stiffly in oilskins.

There was a boy, Jean-Marie, the ship's boy. His father had brought him, leading him by the hand. The sailors jostled him, made fun of his boots, which were too big, and of the tears already welling in his eyes.

The captain was still in his cabin. Finally, he opened the door. He closed it carefully behind him. He was curt, very pale, and his features were drawn.

'Are you the wireless operator? . . . Right. I'll give you your orders in a little while. Meanwhile, take a look round the wireless room.'

Hours passed. Now the boat's owner stood on the quay. Women and mothers were still arriving with parcels for the men who were about to sail.

Fallut shook, fearful for his cabin, whose door was not

to be opened at any price, because Adèle, dishevelled, mouth half open, was sprawled sideways, fast asleep, across the bed.

A touch of the early-morning nausea, which was felt not only by Fallut but by all the men who had toured the bars of the town or travelled there overnight by train.

One by one, they drifted away to the Grand Banks Café, where they drank coffee laced with spirits.

'See you soon! . . . if we come back!'

A loud blast of the ship's horn. Then two more. The women and children, after one last hug, rushing towards the end of the breakwater. The ship's owner shaking Fallut's hand.

The hawsers were cast off. The trawler slid forward, moved clear of the quay. Then Jean-Marie, the ship's boy, choking with fright, stamped his feet in desperation and thought of making a bid to get back to dry land.

Fallut had been sitting where Maigret was sitting now.

'Half ahead! . . . One five-oh turns! . . . Full steam ahead!'

Was Adèle still asleep? Would she be woken up by the first swell and be nervous?

Fallut did not move from the seat which had been his for so many years. Ahead of him was the sea, the Atlantic.

His nerves were taut, for he now realized what a stupid thing he had done. It had not seemed so serious when he was ashore.

'Two points port!'

And then there were shouts, and the group on the breakwater rushed forward. A man, who had clambered up the derrick to wave goodbye to his family, had fallen on to the deck!

'Stop engine! . . . Astern engine! . . . Stop engine!'

There was no sign of life from the cabin. Wasn't there still time to put the woman ashore?

Rowing boats approached the vessel, which was now stationary between the jetties. A fishing boat was asking for right of way.

But the man was injured. He would have to be left behind. He was lowered into a dinghy.

The women were demoralized. They were deeply superstitious.

On top of which the ship's boy had to be restrained from jumping into the water because he was so terrified of leaving!

'Ahead steam! . . . Half! . . . Full! . . .'

Le Clinche was settling into his workplace, headphones on head, testing the instruments. And there, in his domain, he was writing:

My Darling Girl,
    It's eight in the morning! We're off. Already we can't see the town and . . .

Maigret lit a fresh pipe and got to his feet so that he would have a better view of his surroundings.

He was in full possession of the characters in the case and, in a sense, was now able to move them around like counters on the boat which lay spread out before him.

'First meal in the narrow officers' mess: Fallut, the first

mate, the chief mechanic and the wireless operator. The captain announces that henceforth he will be taking all his meals in his cabin, alone.'

They have never heard the like of it! Such an outlandish idea! They all try in vain to come up with a reason for it.

Maigret, clasping his hand to his forehead, muttered:

'It's the ship's boy's job to take the captain his food. The captain opens the door only part of the way or else hides Adèle under the bed, which he has propped up.'

The two of them have to make do with a meal for one. The first time, the woman laughs. And no doubt Fallut leaves nearly all his share to her.

He is too solemn. She makes fun of him. She is nice to him. He unbends. He smiles.

And up in the foredeck are they not already muttering about the evil eye? Aren't they talking about the captain's decision to eat by himself? And moreover, who ever saw a captain walking around with the key to his cabin in his pocket!

The twin screws turn. The trawler has acquired the sense of unease which will continue to fill it for three months.

Below deck, men like Louis shovel coal into the maw of the furnaces for eight or ten hours a day or keep a drowsy eye on the oil-pressure gauge.

Three days. That's the general view. It has taken just three days to create an atmosphere of anxiety. And it was at that point that the crew began wondering if Fallut was mad.

Why? Was it jealousy? But Adèle stated that she didn't see Le Clinche until about day four.

Until then, he is too busy with his new equipment. He tunes in and listens, for his personal satisfaction. He makes trial transmissions. And with his headphones constantly on his head, he writes page after page as if the postman was standing by to whisk his letters away and deliver them to his fiancée.

Three days. Hardly time to get to know one another. Perhaps the chief mechanic, peering through portholes, has caught sight of the young woman? But he never mentioned it.

The atmosphere on board builds only gradually as the crew are drawn together through shared adventures. But as yet there are no adventures to share. They have not yet even started to fish. For that they must wait until they reach the Grand Banks, yonder, off Newfoundland, on the other side of the Atlantic, where they will not be for another ten days yet, at the earliest.

Maigret was standing on the bridge, and any man waking then and seeing him would have wondered what he was doing there, an imposing, solitary figure calmly surveying his surroundings.

And what was he doing? He was trying to understand! All the characters were in position, each with a particular outlook and all with their own preoccupations.

But after this point, there was no way of guessing the rest. There was a large gap. The inspector had only witnesses to rely upon.

'It was on about the third day out that Captain Fallut and the wireless operator started thinking of each other as enemies. Each had a revolver in his pocket. They seemed afraid of each other.'

Yet Le Clinche was not yet Adèle's lover!

'But from that moment, the captain behaved as if he was mad.'

They are now in the middle of the Atlantic. They have left the regular lanes used by the great liners. Now they hardly ever sight even other trawlers, English or German, as they steam towards their fishing grounds.

Does Adèle start to grumble and complain about being cooped up?

. . . *wondered if he wasn't actually mad* . . .

Everyone agrees that mad is the right word. And it seems unlikely that Adèle alone is responsible for bringing about such an astonishing change in a well-adjusted man who has always made a religion of order.

She has not deceived him yet! He has allowed her two or three turns around the deck, at night, provided she takes multiple precautions.

So why is he behaving as if he is *actually mad*?

Here the evidence of witnesses begins to mount up:

'He gives the order to anchor the trawler in a position where for as long as anyone can remember no one ever caught a single cod . . .'

He is not an excitable man or a fool, nor does he lose his temper easily! He is a steady, upstanding citizen of careful habits who for a time dreamed of sharing his life with his landlady, Madame Bernard, and of ending his days in the house full of embroidery in Rue d'Étretat.

'There's one accident after another. When we finally

get on to the Banks and start catching fish, it gets salted in such a way that it's going bad by the time we get back.'

Fallut is no novice! He's about to retire. Until now, no one has ever had reason to question his competence.

He takes all his meals in his cabin.

'He doesn't talk to me,' Adèle will say. 'He goes for days, weeks sometimes, without saying a word to me. And then suddenly it comes over him again . . .'

A sudden wave of sensuality! She's there! In his cabin! He shares her bed! And for weeks on end he manages to stay at arm's length until the temptation proves too strong!

Would he behave this way if his only grievance was jealousy?

The chief mechanic prowls round the cabin, licking his lips. But he doesn't have the nerve to force the lock.

And finally, the Epilogue. The *Océan* is on the way home to France, laden with badly salted cod.

Is it during the voyage back that the captain draws up what is virtually his will in which he says no one should be accused of causing his death?

If so, he clearly wants to die. He intends to kill himself. No one on board, except him, is capable of taking a ship's bearings, and he has enough of the seafaring spirit to bring his boat back to port first.

Kill himself because he has infringed regulations by taking a woman to sea with him?

Kill himself because insufficient salt was used on the fish, which will sell for a few francs below the market rate?

Kill himself because the crew, bewildered by his odd conduct, believe that he is a lunatic?

The captain, the most cool-headed, the most scrupulously careful master in all Fécamp? The same man whose log books are held up as models?

The man who for so long has been living in the peaceful house of Madame Bernard?

The steam vessel docks. The members of the crew rush on shore and make a bee-line for the Grand Banks Café, where they can at last get a proper drink.

And every man jack of them is stamped with the mark of mystery! On certain questions they all remain silent. They are all on edge.

Is it because a captain has behaved in ways that no one understands?

Fallut goes on shore alone. He will have to wait until the quays are deserted before he can disembark Adèle.

He takes a few steps forwards. Two men are hiding: the wireless operator and Gaston Buzier, the girl's lover.

But the captain is jumped by a third man, who strangles him and drops his body into the harbour.

And all this happened at the very spot where the *Océan* is now gently rocking on the black water. The body had got tangled in the anchor chain.

Maigret was smoking. He scowled.

'Even at the first interview, Le Clinche lies when he talks about a man wearing tan-coloured shoes who killed Fallut. Now the man with the tan-coloured shoes is Buzier. When he is brought face to face with him, Le Clinche retracts his statement.'

Why would he lie about this if not to protect a third

person, in other words the murderer? And why wouldn't Le Clinche name him?

He does no such thing. He even lets himself be put behind bars instead of him. He makes little effort to defend himself, even though there is every likelihood that he will go down for murder.

He is grim, like a man riddled with guilt. He does not dare look either his fiancée or Maigret in the eye.

One small detail. Before returning to the trawler, he headed back to the Grand Banks Café. He went up to his room. He burned a number of papers.

When he gets out of jail, he isn't happy, even though Marie Léonnec is there, encouraging him to look on the bright side. And somehow he manages to get hold of a revolver.

He is afraid. He hesitates. For a long time he just sits there, eyes closed, finger on the trigger.

And then he fires.

As the night wore on, it turned cooler, and the smell of seaweed and iodine weighed more strongly on the breeze.

The trawler had risen by several metres. The deck was now level with the quayside, and the push and drag of the tide caused the boat to buck sideways and made the gangway creak.

Maigret had forgotten how tired he was. The hardest time was over. It would soon be dawn.

He summarized:

Captain Fallut, who had been retrieved dead from the anchor chain.

Adèle and Gaston Buzier, who argued all the time, reached the stage where they could not stand each other and yet had no one else to turn to.

Le Clinche, who had been wheeled out on a trolley, swathed in white, from the operating theatre.

And Marie Léonnec . . .

Not forgetting the men in the Grand Banks Café, who, even when drunk, seemed haunted by painful memories . . .

'The third day!' Maigret said aloud. 'That's where I need to look!'

Something much worse than jealousy . . . *But something which flowed directly from the presence of Adèle on board the boat.*

The effort took it out of him. The effect of the strain on all his mental faculties. The boat rocked gently. A light came on in the foredeck, where the sailors were about to get up.

'The third day . . .'

His throat contracted. He looked down on the afterdeck and then along the quay, where, hours before, a man had leaned over and brandished a fist.

Maybe it was partly the effect of the cold and maybe not. But either way he suddenly shivered.

'The third day . . . The ship's boy, Jean-Marie, who kicked up a fuss because he did not want to go to sea, was swept overboard by a wave, at night . . .'

Maigret's eye ran round the whole deck, as if trying to determine where the accident had happened.

'There were only two witnesses, Captain Fallut and the

wireless operator, Pierre Le Clinche. The next day or the day after that, Le Clinche became Adèle's lover!'

It was a turning point! Maigret did not loiter for another second. Someone was stirring in the foredeck. No one saw him stride across the plank connecting the boat to dry land.

With his hands in his pockets, his nose blue with the cold, unsmiling, he returned to the Hôtel de la Plage.

It was not yet light. Yet it was no longer night because, out at sea, the crests of waves were picked out in crude white. And gulls were light flecks against the sky.

A train whistled in the station. An old woman set out for the rocks, a basket on her back and a hook in her hand, to look for crabs.

10. *What Happened on the Third Day*

When Maigret left his room and came downstairs at around eight that morning, his head felt empty and his chest woolly, the way a man feels when he has drunk too much.

'Aren't things going the way you'd like?' asked his wife.

He had given a shrug, and she had not insisted. But there on the terrace of the hotel, facing a frothing, sly-green sea, he found Marie Léonnec. And she was not alone. There was a man sitting at her table. She stood up quickly and stammered to the inspector:

'May I introduce my father? He's just got here.'

The wind was cool, the sky overcast. The gulls skimmed the tops of the water.

'An honour to meet you, sir. Deeply honoured and most happy . . .'

Maigret looked at him without enthusiasm. He was short and would not have been any more ridiculous to look at than the next man but for his nose, which was disproportionately large, being the size of three normal noses and, furthermore, was stippled, like a strawberry.

It wasn't his fault. But it was a physical affliction. And it was all anyone saw. When he spoke it was the only thing people looked at, so that it was impossible to feel any sympathy for him.

'You must join us in a little . . . ?'

'Thank you, no. I've just had breakfast.'

'Perhaps a small glass of something, to warm the cockles?'

'No, really.'

He was insistent. Is it not a form of politeness to make people drink when they don't want to?

Maigret observed him and observed his daughter, who, apart from that nose, bore him a strong resemblance. By looking at her in this light, he was able to get a picture of what she would be like in a dozen years, when the bloom of youth had faded.

'I'll come straight to the point, inspector. That's my motto, and I've travelled all night to do just that. When Jorissen came to me and said that he would accompany my daughter, I gave him my permission. So I don't think anyone could say that I am at all narrow-minded.'

Unfortunately Maigret was anxious to be elsewhere. Then there was the nose. And also the pompous tone of the middle-class worthy who likes the sound of his own voice.

'Even so, it's my duty as a father to keep myself fully informed, don't you agree? Which is why I'm asking you to tell me, in your heart and conscience, if you think this young man is innocent.'

Marie Léonnec did not know where to look. She must have known deep down that her father's initiative was unlikely to help arrange matters.

As long as she had been by herself, rushing to the aid of her fiancé, she had seemed rather admirable. Or at any rate she made a touching figure.

But now, inside the family, it was another matter. There

was more than a whiff here of the shop back in Quimper, the discussions which had preceded her departure, the tittle-tattle of the neighbours.

'Are you asking me if he killed Captain Fallut?'

'Yes. You must understand that it is essential that . . .'

Maigret stared straight in front of him in his most detached manner.

'Well . . .'

He noticed the girl's hands, which were shaking.

'No, he didn't kill him. Now, if you'll excuse me, there's something I really must attend to. I shall doubtless have the pleasure of meeting up with you later . . .'

Then he turned tail! He fled so fast that he knocked over a chair on the terrace. He assumed that father and daughter were startled but did not turn round to find out.

Once on the quay, he followed the paved walkway. The *Océan* was some distance away. Even so, he noticed that a number of men had arrived with their sailor's kitbags slung over their shoulders and were getting their first sight of the boat. A cart was unloading bags of potatoes. The company's man was there with his polished boots and his pencil behind his ear.

There was a great deal of noise coming from the Grand Banks Café. Its doors were open, and Maigret could just make out Louis holding forth in the middle of a circle of the 'new' men.

He did not stop. Though he saw the landlord making a sign to him, he hurried on his way. Five minutes later he was ringing the bell of the hospital.

*

The registrar was very young. Visible under his white coat were a suit in the latest fashion and an elegant tie.

'The wireless operator? It was I who took his temperature and pulse this morning. He's doing as well as can be expected.'

'Has he come round?'

'Oh yes! He hasn't spoken to me, but his eyes followed me around all the time.'

'Is it all right if I talk to him about important matters?'

The registrar waved a hand vaguely, an indifferent gesture.

'Don't see why not. If the operation has been a success and he hasn't got a temperature, then . . . You want to see him?'

Pierre Le Clinche was by himself in a small room with distempered walls. The air was hot and humid. He watched Maigret coming towards him. His eyes were bright, and there was not a trace of anxiety in them.

'As you see, he's making excellent progress. He'll be on his feet in a week. On the other hand, there's a chance that he'll be left with a limp, for a tendon in his hip was severed. And he'll have to take care. Would you prefer it if I leave you alone with him?'

It was really quite disconcerting. The previous evening, a bleeding, unwholesome mess had been brought which could not possibly, it seemed, have harboured the faintest breath of life.

And now Maigret found a white bed, a face that was slightly drawn and a little pale which was more tranquil now than he had ever seen it. And there was what looked like serenity in those eyes.

That is perhaps why he hesitated. He paced up and down the room, leaned his head for a moment against the double window, from which he could see the port and the trawler, where men in red jerkins were busily moving about.

'Do you feel strong enough to talk to me?' he growled, firing the question without warning as he turned to face the bed.

Le Clinche assented with a faint nod of his head.

'You are aware that I am not officially involved in this case? My friend Jorissen asked me to prove your innocence. It is done. You are not the killer of Captain Fallut.'

He sighed deeply. Then, to get it over with, he put his head down and charged:

'Tell me the truth about what happened on the third day out, I mean about the death of Jean-Marie.'

He avoided looking directly at the patient. He filled a pipe as a way of appearing casual and when the silence went on and on, he murmured:

'It was evening. There were only Captain Fallut and you on deck. Were you standing together?'

'No!'

'The captain was walking near the afterdeck?'

'Yes. I'd just left my cabin. He didn't see me. I watched him because I felt there was something odd about the way he was behaving.'

'You didn't know at that point that there was a woman on board?'

'No! I thought that if he was being so careful about keeping his door locked, it was because he was storing smuggled goods inside.'

The voice was weary. And yet, it became suddenly more emphatic for he said distinctly:

'It was the most terrible thing I ever saw, inspector! Who talked? Tell me!'

And he closed his eyes, exactly as he had as he sat waiting for the moment when he would fire a bullet through his pocket into his belly.

'Nobody. The captain was strolling on deck, feeling apprehensive no doubt, just as he had ever since he'd left port. Was there anybody at the wheel?'

'A helmsman. He couldn't see us because it was dark.'

'The ship's boy showed up . . .'

Le Clinche interrupted him by heaving himself half up, both hands gripping the rope hanging from the ceiling which enabled him to change his position.

'Where's Marie?'

'At the hotel. Her father has just come.'

'To take her back! Fair enough. He should take her home. But whatever happens, she mustn't come here!'

He was getting worked up. His voice was flatter and its flow more broken.

Maigret could sense that his temperature was climbing. His eyes were becoming unnaturally bright.

'I don't know who has been talking to you. But it's time I told you everything.'

His agitation had reached such a pitch, and was so vehement, that he looked and sounded as if he was almost raving.

'It was awful! You never saw the kid. Skinny's not the word. Wore clothes made from an old cut-down canvas suit of his father's . . . On the first day, he'd been scared and he blubbed. How can I explain . . . Afterwards he got his own back by playing nasty tricks on people. What do you expect at his age? Do you know what *a little brat* is? Well, that was him. Twice I caught him reading the letters I wrote to my fiancée. He'd just look me brazenly in the eye and say:

'"Writing to your bit of fluff?"

'That evening . . . I think the captain was walking up and down because he was too jumpy to sleep. There was quite a swell on. From time to time, a green sea would wash over the foredeck rail and flood across the metal plates of the deck. But it wasn't a storm.

'I was maybe ten metres from them. I only heard a few words but I could see their shapes. The kid was on his high horse, he was laughing. And the captain stood there, his neck sunk in his jerkin and his hands in his pockets . . .

'Jean-Marie had talked about my "bit of fluff" and he must have been taking the same sort of rise out of Fallut. He had a piercing voice. I remember catching a couple of words:

'"And if I ever told everybody how . . ."

'I didn't understand until later . . . He'd found out that the captain was hiding a woman in his cabin. He was full of himself. There was a swagger about him. He wasn't aware of how vindictive he was being.

'Then this is what happened. The captain raised one hand to give him a cuff over the ear. The kid was very nimble and ducked. Then he shouted something, probably another threat about telling what he knew.

'Fallut's hand struck a rigging stay. It must have hurt like the devil. He saw red.

'It was the fable of the lion and the gnat all over again. Forgetting he was a ship's master, he started chasing the kid. At first, the boy ran off laughing. The captain started to panic.

'A chance remark and anyone who heard it would know everything. Fallut was out of his mind with fear.

'I saw him reach out to catch Jean-Marie by the shoulders, but instead of grabbing hold of him he pushed him over, head first . . .

'That's it. Fatalities occur. His head collided with a capstan. I heard the sound, it was awful, a dull thud. *His skull . . .*'

He held both hands up to his face. He was deathly pale. Sweat streamed down his forehead.

'A big wave swept over the deck at that moment. So it was a waterlogged body that the captain bent down to examine. At the same time, he caught sight of me. I don't think it crossed my mind to hide. I started walking towards him. I got there just in time to see the boy's body clench and then stiffen in a reflex that I'll never forget.

'Dead! It was so senseless! The two of us looked at each other, not taking it in, unable to understand what an appalling thing had happened.

'No one else had seen or heard anything. Fallut didn't dare touch the boy. It was me who felt his chest, his hands and that crumpled skull. There was no blood. No wound. Just the skull, which had cracked.

'We stayed there for maybe a quarter of an hour, not knowing what to do, grim, shoulders frozen, while at intervals the spray lashed our faces.

'The captain was not the same man. It was as if something inside him had been broken too.

'When he spoke, his voice was sharp, without warmth.

'"The crew mustn't learn the truth! Bad for ship's discipline."

'And while I looked on, he himself picked the boy up. Then just one more effort. Though . . . though I do remember that with his thumb he made the sign of the cross on the boy's forehead.

'The body, which had been snatched by the sea, was swept back twice against the hull. Both of us were still standing in the dark. We did not dare look at each other. We didn't dare speak.'

Maigret had just lit his pipe, clamping his teeth hard on the stem.

A nurse came in. Both men watched her with eyes that seemed so vacant that she was disconcerted and stammered:

'Time to take your temperature.'

'Come back later!'

When the door closed behind her, the inspector asked:

'Was it then that he told you about the woman?'

'From then on, he was never the same again. He probably wasn't certifiably mad. But there was definitely something unhinged about him. He put one hand on my shoulder and murmured:

'"And all because of a woman, young man!"

'I was cold. I was not thinking straight. I couldn't take

my eyes off the sea on the side where the body had been carried away.

'Did they tell you about the captain? A short, lean man with a face full of energy. He usually spoke in terse, unfinished phrases.

'That was it! Fifty-five years old. Coming up to retirement. Solid reputation. A little put by in the bank. All over! Finished! In one minute! Less than a minute. On account of a kid who . . . No, on account of a woman . . .

'And then and there, in the darkness, in a quiet, angry voice, he told me the whole story, bit by bit. A woman from Le Havre. A woman who couldn't have been up to much, he was well aware of that. But he couldn't live without her . . .

'He'd brought her with him. And the moment he did, he had a sudden feeling that her presence on board would mean trouble.

'She was there. Asleep.'

The wireless operator began to fidget restlessly.

'I can't remember everything he told me. For he had this need to talk about her, which he did with a mixture of loathing and passion.'

'"A captain is never justified in causing a scandal likely to undermine his authority."

'I can still hear those words. It was my first time out on a boat and I now thought of the sea as a monster which would swallow us all up.

'Fallut quoted examples. In such a year such and such a captain, who had brought his mistress along with him . . .

There were so many fights on board that three men never came back.

'The wind was strengthening. The spray kept coming at us. From time to time, a wave would lick at our feet which kept sliding on the slippery metal deck.

'He wasn't mad, oh no! But he wasn't Fallut any more either.

'"See this trip through and then we'll see!"

'I didn't understand what he meant. He struck me as being both sensible and freakish, a man still clinging to his sense of duty.

'"No one must know! A captain can never be in the wrong!"

'My nerves were so strung out I was ill with it. I couldn't think any more. My thoughts were all jumbled up in my head, and by the finish it felt as if I was living through a waking nightmare.

'That woman in the cabin, the woman a man like the captain could not live without, the woman whose very name made him catch his breath.

'And there was me writing reams and reams to my fiancée, who I wouldn't be seeing again for three months, and I never felt obsessed, possessed like that! And when he said words like her *flesh* or her *body* I felt my cheeks go hot without knowing why.'

Maigret put the question slowly:

'And no one, apart from the two of you, knew the truth about the death of Jean-Marie?'

'No one!'

'And was it the captain who, in the customary way, read out the prayers for the dead?'

'At first light. The weather had got thick. We were steaming through icy grey mist.'

'Didn't the crew say anything?'

'There were funny looks and some whispering. But Fallut was more authoritarian than ever, and his voice had acquired a new cutting edge. He would not tolerate any answering back. He got angry with anyone who looked at him in a way he didn't like. He spied on the men, as if he was trying to detect any suspicions they might be getting.'

'What about you?'

Le Clinche didn't answer. He stretched out one arm for a glass of water on his bedside table and drank from it greedily.

'So you began prowling round the cabin more often, didn't you? You wanted to see this woman who had got so far under the captain's skin? Did you start the following night?'

'Yes. I ran into her, just for a moment. Then the next night . . . I'd noticed that the key to the wireless room was the same as the key of the cabin. It was the captain's watch. I crept in, like a thief.'

'You went to bed with her?'

The wireless operator's face hardened.

'I swear you won't understand, you can't! The whole atmosphere was nothing like anything that happens in the real world. The kid . . . the previous day's ceremony . . . But whenever I thought about it, the same picture kept surfacing in my mind, the image of a woman unlike any other, a woman whose body, whose flesh could turn a man into something that he was not.'

'She led you on?'

'She was in bed, half-dressed . . .'

He turned bright scarlet. He looked away.

'How long did you stay in the cabin?'

'Maybe a couple of hours, I don't remember. When I left with the blood still pounding in my ears, the captain was there, just outside the door. He didn't say a word. He watched me walk past. I almost went down on my knees so I could say it wasn't my fault and that I was sorry. But he remained stony-faced. I walked on. I returned to my post.

'I was scared. After that, I always went around with my loaded revolver in my pocket because I was convinced he was going to kill me.

'He never spoke to me again, except for ship's business. And even then, most of the time he sent me his orders in writing.

'I wish I could explain it better, but I can't. Each day it got worse. I had a feeling that everybody knew about the terrible thing that happened.

'The chief mechanic went sniffing around the cabin too. The captain stayed inside it for hours and hours.

'The men started giving us inquisitive, anxious looks. They guessed that something was going on. How many times did I hear talk of the evil eye?

'But there was only one thing I wanted . . .'

'Of course there was,' grunted Maigret.

There was a silence. Le Clinche stared at the inspector with eyes full of resentment.

'We ran into bad weather, ten days on the trot. I was seasick. But I kept thinking about her. She was . . . fragrant! She . . . I can't explain. It was like a pain. That's it! A desire capable of inflicting pain, of making me weep tears of rage! Especially when I saw the captain go into his cabin. Because now, I could imagine . . . You see, she'd called me her *big boy*! In a special voice, sort of breathy. I kept saying those two words over and over to torture myself. I stopped writing to Marie. I built impossible dreams: I'd run away with that woman the moment we got back to Fécamp.'

'What about the captain?'

'He got even more stony-faced and brusque. Maybe there was a touch of madness about him after all, I don't know. He gave orders that we were to fish at some location or other, and all the old hands claimed no one had ever seen a fish in those waters. He refused to have his orders questioned. He was afraid of me. Did he know I had a gun? He had one too. Whenever we met, he kept his hand near his pocket. I kept trying to see Adèle again. But he was always around, with bags under his eyes and his lips drawn back. And the stink of cod. The men who were salting the fish down in the hold . . . There was one accident after another.

'And the chief mechanic was also on the prowl. It got so that none of us spoke freely any more. We were like three lunatics. There were nights when I believe I could have killed somebody to get to her. Can you understand that? Nights when I tore my handkerchief to shreds with my teeth while I repeated over and over, in the same voice that she had used:

'"*My big boy! That's my big fool!*"

'How long it seemed! Each night was followed by a new day! And then more days! And with nothing but grey water around us, freezing fogs, fish-scales and cod guts everywhere!

'A taste of pickling brine in the back of the throat that made your stomach heave . . .

'Just that once! I believe that if I could have gone to her one more time I'd have been cured! But it was impossible. *He* was there. He was always there, more hollow-eyed all the time.

'The constant pitching and tossing, with nothing as far as the eye could see. And then we saw cliffs!

'Can you grasp the fact that it had been like that for three months? Well, instead of being cured, I was even sicker. It's only now that I'm beginning to realize that it was a sickness.

'I hated the captain who was always in my way. I detested that man who was already old and kept a woman like Adèle under lock and key.

'I was afraid of returning to port. I was afraid of losing her for ever.

'By the finish, I was as scared of him as of the devil himself! Yes, as if he were some kind of evil genie who was keeping the woman all to himself!

'As we got in, there were a few navigation errors. Then the men jumped ashore, relieved to be back, and headed straight for the bars. But I knew the captain was only waiting for the cover of night to get Adèle off the boat.

'I went back to my room over Léon's bar. There were old letters, photos of my fiancée and the like, and I don't know why but I got into a vile temper and I burned the whole lot.

'Then I went back out. I wanted her! I'll say it again: I wanted her! Hadn't she told me that when we got back Fallut would marry her?

'I bumped into a man . . .'

He let himself slump back on to his pillow, and on his tortured features appeared an expression of agonized torment.

'Because you know . . .' he gasped.

'Yes. Jean-Marie's father. The trawler was berthed. Only the captain and Adèle were still on board. He was about to bring her out. And then . . .'

'Please, no more!'

'And then you told the man who had come to look at the boat on which his boy had died that his son had been murdered. True? And you followed him. You were hiding behind a truck when he went up to the captain . . .'

'Stop!'

'The murder happened there, while you watched.'

'Please stop!'

'No! You were there when it happened. Then you went on board and let the woman out.'

'I didn't want her any more!'

From outside came a long blast of a hooter. Le Clinche's lips trembled as he stammered:

'The *Océan* . . .'

'That's right. She sails at high tide.'

Neither of them spoke. They could hear all the sounds made in the hospital, down to the muffled swish of a patient's trolley being wheeled to the operating theatre.

'I didn't want her any more!' the wireless operator repeated wildly.

'But it was too late!'

There was another silence. Then Le Clinche's voice came again:

'And yet . . . now . . . I want so much to . . .'

He did not dare pronounce the word that stuck to his tongue.

'Live?'

Then he went on:

'Don't you understand? I was mad. I don't understand it myself. It all happened elsewhere, in another world . . . Then we got back here, and I realized what had been happening. Listen. There was that dark cabin and men prowling round, and nothing else existed. I felt as if that was my whole life! I longed to hear those words again, *my big boy!* I couldn't even begin to say how it all happened. I opened the door. She slipped out. There was a man in tan-coloured shoes waiting for her, and they started hugging each other on the side of the quay.

'And I woke up – it's the only word for it. And ever since all I've wanted is not to die. Marie Léonnec came with you to see me. Adèle came too, with that other man.'

'What do you want me to say?'

'It's too late now, isn't it? I was let out of jail. I went on board and got my revolver. Marie was waiting for me by the boat. She didn't know . . .

'And that same afternoon, that woman was there, talking. And the man in the tan-coloured shoes . . .

'Who could possibly make sense of it all? I pulled the trigger. It took me an age to bring myself to do it, on account of Marie Léonnec, who was there!

'And now . . .'

He sobbed. Then he literally screamed:

'All the same, I've got to die! And I don't want to die! I'm afraid of dying! I . . . I . . .'

His body was racked by such spasms that Maigret called a nurse, who quietly and unfussily subdued him with an economical ease born of long professional experience.

The trawler gave a second harrowing summons on its hooter, and the women hurried down to line the jetty.

11. *The* Océan *Sails*

Maigret reached the quay just as the new captain was about to give the order to cast off the hawsers. He caught sight of the chief mechanic, who was saying goodbye to his wife. He went up to him and took him to one side.

'Something I need to know. It was you, wasn't it, who found the captain's will and dropped it into the police station letterbox?'

The man looked worried and hesitated.

'You've nothing to worry about. You suspected Le Clinche. You thought that it was a way of saving his neck. Even though you both had had your eye on the same woman.'

The hooter, peremptory now, barked at the latecomers, and hugging couples on the quayside peeled away from each other.

'Don't bring all that up again, do you mind? Is it true that he's going to die?'

'Unless we can save him. Where was the will?'

'Among the captain's papers.'

'What exactly were you looking for?'

'I was hoping to find a photo,' the man said, lowering his eyes. 'Look, let me go, I've got to . . .'

The hawser fell into the water. The gangway was being raised. The chief mechanic jumped on to the deck, gave his wife a last wave and cast a final look at Maigret.

Then the trawler headed slowly towards the harbour entrance. A sailor lifted the ship's boy, who was barely fifteen, on to his shoulders. The boy had got hold of the man's pipe and was proudly clenching it between his teeth.

On the land, women were weeping.

By walking quickly, they could follow the vessel, which did not pick up speed until it was clear of the jetties. Some voices were shouting out reminders:

'If you come across the *Atlantique*, don't forget to tell Dugodet that his wife . . .'

The sky was still low and threatening. The wind pressed down on the water, ruckling its surface and raising small white-crested waves, which made an angry washing sound.

A Parisian in whites was taking photos of the departing trawler. He had two little girls in white dresses in tow. They were laughing.

Maigret collided with a woman, almost knocking her over. She clutched his arm and asked:

'Well? Is he better?'

It was Adèle, who hadn't powdered her nose since at least that morning, and the skin of her face was shiny.

'Where's Buzier?' asked the inspector.

'He said he'd rather go back to Le Havre. He doesn't want any trouble. Anyway, I said I was finishing with him. But what about that boy, Le Clinche?'

'Don't know.'

'Go on, you can tell me!'

Absolutely not. He turned and left her standing there. He'd picked out a group on the jetty: Marie Léonnec, her father and Madame Maigret. All three were facing in the direction of the trawler which for a moment drew level with them. Marie Léonnec was saying fervently:

'That's *his* boat!'

Maigret slowly walked towards them, in a surly mood. His wife was the first to spot him among the crowd which had gathered to see the trawler set off for the Grand Banks.

'Did he pull through?'

Monsieur Léonnec, looking anxious, turned his misshapen nose in his direction.

'Ah! I'm so glad to see you. Where are you with your inquiries, inspector?'

'Nowhere.'

'Meaning?'

'Nothing . . . I don't know.'

Marie opened her eyes wide.

'But Pierre?'

'The operation was a success. It seems he'll be all right.'

'He's innocent, isn't he? Oh please! Tell my father he didn't do it!'

She put her whole heart into the words. Contemplating her, he saw how she would be in ten years' time, with the same look as her father, a somewhat overbearing manner ideally suited to dealing with customers in the shop.

'He didn't kill the captain.'

Turning to his wife:

'I've just had a telegram calling me back to Paris.'

'So soon? I'd promised to go swimming tomorrow with . . .'

She caught his eye and understood.

'If you'll excuse us.'

'We'll walk back to the hotel with you.'

Maigret saw Jean-Marie's father, dead drunk, still bran-dishing his fist at the trawler, and looked away.

'Don't put yourselves out, please.'

'Tell me,' said Monsieur Léonnec, 'do you think I could arrange for him to be transferred to Quimper? People are bound to talk.'

Marie looked pleadingly at him. She was very pale. She said in a faltering voice:

'After all, he is innocent,'

'I don't know. You are better placed . . .'

'But at least you must allow me to offer you something? A bottle of champagne?'

'No thanks.'

'Just a glass of something? Benedictine, for example, since we're in the town where . . .'

'A beer, then.'

Upstairs, Madame Maigret was shutting their cases.

'So you share my opinion, then. He's a fine boy who . . .'

She still had that little-girl look about her! The look that pleaded with him to say yes!

'I think he'll make a good husband.'

'And be a good hand at business!' said her father, going one better. 'Because I won't have him sailing the high seas for months on end. When a man's married, he has a responsibility to . . .'

'Goes without saying.'

'Especially since I have no son. Surely you can under-stand that!'

'Of course.'

Maigret was keeping an eye on the stairs. Eventually, his wife appeared.

'The luggage is all ready. They say there's not a train until . . .'

'Doesn't matter. We'll hire a car.'

It was a getaway!

'If ever you have occasion to be in Quimper . . .'

'Yes, yes . . .'

And the way the girl looked at him! She seemed to have understood that things were not all as straightforward as they seemed, but her eyes pleaded with Maigret not to say any more.

She wanted her fiancé.

The inspector shook hands all round, paid the bill and finished his beer.

'Thank you so much Detective Chief Inspector Maigret.'

'There really is no need.'

The car which had been hired by phone arrived.

*

so unless you have come up with something which I have missed, I shall sign off with a recommendation that the case be closed.

This was a passage from a letter sent by Chief Inspector Grenier, of the Le Havre Police, to Maigret, who replied by telegraph:

Agreed.

Six months later, he was sent a card through the post, which said:

Madame Le Clinche has great pleasure in announcing the wedding of her son, Pierre, and Mademoiselle Marie Léonnec, which . . .

And shortly afterwards, when in connection with another inquiry he was looking round a certain kind of establishment in Rue Pasquier, he thought he recognized a young woman who looked quickly away.

Adèle!

And that was all. Or not quite. Five years later, Maigret was on a short visit to Quimper. He saw the proprietor of a chandler's shop, standing in his doorway. He was still a young man, very tall with the beginnings of a paunch.

He walked with a slight limp. He called to a toddler of three, who was playing with his top on the pavement.

'Come in now, Pierrot. Your mother will be cross!'

The man, too preoccupied with his offspring, did not recognize Maigret, who in any case quickened his step, looked away and pulled a wry face.